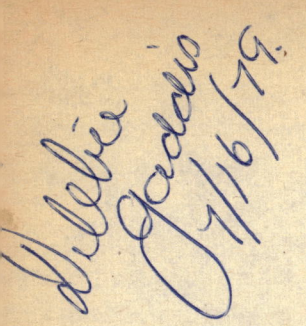

THE END OF AN AFFAIR

When Shane had come to Shadow Lake she had been very certain she was going to ask Court for a divorce. That he would be angry, his pride hurt, she knew, but she wondered wearily if he, too, might not be relieved to have the whole sorry business over with.

Now she was going back to him and she could not be certain when she had reached that decision or what had brought her to it.

If there *was* a future for her with Jeff Kendall, then what might have been her decision? Not to leave Court at all. To simply give up on a failing marriage is one thing. To leave for another man, to end ten years of marriage with the same betrayal that had sent his mother to her death — she could never do that to Court.

But wouldn't Court say that she had already betrayed him?

What Price Love
By Alice Lent Covert

ZEBRA BOOKS
KENSINGTON PUBLISHING CORP.

ZEBRA BOOKS

are published by

KENSINGTON PUBLISHING CORP.
21 East 40th Street
New York, N.Y. 10016

Copyright © 1979 by Alice Lent Covert

All rights reserved. No part of this book may be reproduced in any form or by any means without the prior written consent of the Publisher, excepting brief quotes used in reviews.

First Printing: June, 1979

Printed in the United States of America

What Price Love
1.
(Casey)

The telephone rang at seven in the morning. Megan Casey stirred and reached out to the bedside table for the instrument, muttering a sleepy greeting. "What's with the cock-a-doodle bit, Jeff? It's the middle of the night."

"Sorry about that. I came in late last night and I'm getting ready to drive back to the lake now. I wanted to catch you at home."

"All right, you've caught me."

You could have caught me last night and I wouldn't have cared how late it was; you knew that.

"I'll be down again in the morning. I'm seeing a friend off on the early flight."

"Oh?" He's sending his lady love back to her husband. Dear, kind Lord, let it be that!

"I'll be free by ten and I thought we might get some work done for a change."

"Hey!" Casey lifted herself to an elbow and glared into the transmitter. "*I'm* not the one who's been trundling off up to Shadow Lake for weeks on end to fish, or—" her voice changed inflection only slightly, "—whatever the hell it is you've been doing up there."

"Who," Helene Amboy had demanded of Casey recently, "is the young woman Doctor Kendall has been seeing so much of?"

Helene was the wife of one of the psychology professors under Jeff Kendall at Tarant College, the one most likely to succeed him as head of the department if Jeff's nonadmirers managed to get the skids under him.

"Rolfe and I have run into them twice having dinner up at Shadow Lake Inn and other people have seen them, too. She isn't the type one would expect him to be seriously interested in; rather a plain little thing, actually, but he is terribly attentive to her."

Casey gave her no satisfaction. There was, in fact, nothing she could tell her. For the past month or longer Jeff had been spending much of his time in the mountains, at a cabin belonging to his uncle, ostensibly working on a manuscript. He came down for his Monday and Thursday lectures, picked up his mail, checked in briefly with Casey at the office and was gone again. If he had been seeing someone it was news to Casey—not exactly the glad-tidings sort of thing, but news.

Helene's regard was one of watchful curiosity, making careful note of Casey's reaction, if any. Casey took care not to react.

Helene knows about Jeff and me, of course. At least, she guesses. What is it about a woman, if she's in love with a guy and sleeping with him, the last person in the world she can fool is another woman?

She said, coolly, "I am Doctor Kendall's secretary but that doesn't mean I keep track of quite all his appointments," and Helene smiled.

"No, I daresay not."

Helene's bloodhound instincts helped her unearth further information which she happily passed on to Casey. The woman was married, she was about Casey's age, she was Shane Manning, the niece of a former Tarant theology dean. Several years ago she had run away with a boy named Court Manning whose family was involved in some sort of scandal—a young student who had been booted out of the theological seminary.

"Some men might find her attractive, I suppose. She's one of those fragile-looking little things, and she does have lovely eyes. They say she was a bright student, very talented. Her parents were *the* John and Margot Parker, you know."

Casey did not know. She had never heard of John and Margot Parker.

"But you must have! John was the younger brother of Dean Gregory Parker. He was well known as a journalist and photographer, and both he and Margot were very big on the lecture circuit. *Brilliant* people. I must say their daughter doesn't look the intellectual type, but she obviously has some sort of appeal for Doctor Kendall, if you know what I mean."

Casey refrained from saying, I know what you mean and I know why you are telling me these things and kindly just shut the hell up by the simple expedient of clamping her teeth together so tightly her jaws ached.

A married woman, former Tarant girl with roots in Tarant's moldy academic traditions—Doctor Jeffrey Kendall must be out of his cotton-picking mind!

Into the telephone now she said with mock servility, "To hear you is to obey, *effendi*. Where do you want to work, the office or here? Tomorrow is Saturday, and the month's end, and the custodians will be wanting to do the floors and windows—".

Get the guy up here, into the hay if possible, and work can wait a little longer.

"Your place. We've a lot of catching up to do."

Yes, indeedy!

"I'll bring along my latest notes and maybe we can whip them into some sort of shape."

"Roger." Casey grinned sourly. So much for sex.

"Sorry to give you such short notice. I hope you hadn't made other plans for tomorrow."

"No plans. See you in the morning."

Actually, she thought with an upsurge of cheerfulness, he sounded pretty much the way he always did. If his manner was brusque, well then, Jeff always tended to become slightly military when he was preparing to plunge himself and Casey into an arduous session of work.

Even if the rumors were true about him and this Shane Manning, whoever and whatever the lady might be, the home team still had a few things going for it. Jeff was not the marrying kind, so inasmuch as the lady already had a husband, the friendship, of whatever type and temperature, couldn't be of a very permanent nature.

A friend, he had said, and maybe that was the size of it. If she was flying away in the morning that should leave the field clear. Casey was fairly good at holding her own, or at least she always had been. Publicly, her own position where Jeff was concerned was an acceptable one. Unmarried, he needed someone to act as his hostess on the rare occasions when he entertained, or to escort to functions where couples were the order. For two years that someone had been Megan Casey, his attractive (she made herself a small bow) secretary. In those two years, if he had so much as taken anyone else out to dinner, the campus wives had missed it, and this Casey considered highly unlikely.

Up to now Jeff wasn't the marrying kind, but who's to say someone mightn't come along who could change his thinking? Married ladies have been known to get divorces, right? Then what's the home team got going for it?

She slid out of bed and went into the

bathroom, to eye herself in the mirror with displeasure. "You," she said aloud, "are weak. When you learn to tell Doctor Jeffrey Kendall to go straight to hell, and mean it, I will be proud of you. Until then, kindly stay out of my sight as much as possible."

If one looked at it squarely, Jeff owed her nothing—certainly not to come running to report if he took someone out just to make certain she heard it from him first. Megan Casey and Jeff Kendall were both liberated souls, but they believed in fair play. Being serious about each other was hardly a game for three people, and Jeff had not come to Casey to say he'd gotten serious about anyone, had he?

So what's your problem?

My problem is that Jeff hasn't been coming to me at all these past few weeks, and now I'm scared to death of what he may have to tell me when he does come.

She dressed, listening idly to the sounds of the world outside. Below her apartment windows the early morning traffic of Central Street slid past, coming up to her with a muted quality. She liked it. Actually, she liked the town, a fact which always surprised her a bit. It was a nowhere place, tucked away in a green basin amid foothills which climbed northward into towering pine-clad mountains—an outdated town, cradling the outdated college where Casey worked, a cluster of ugly brick buildings arranged about a quadrangle, crisscrossed at right angles by wide tree-sheltered walks. At one corner of the quadrangle stood a white ivy-covered chapel with a finger-pointing-heavenward steeple. The whole thing, Casey often thought amusedly, was straight out of one of those movie sets one saw on the late late show. It was a peaceful-looking picture-postcard kind of *pretty*, which was deceptive, because beneath the calm lay the wrangling, the gossip and conniving, and nasty little bigotries, just as anywhere. One might think that the people who ran an institution of higher learning would of necessity be emotionally mature, sensible adults who walked like they talked, but in Tarant, at any rate, the precise opposite often seemed to Casey to be the fact.

Tarant—college and town—was old, its years deep-rooted in tradition which it kept stubbornly alive. Its people loved Tarant; its fathers and grandfathers had loved it; its great-grandfathers had built it. There was about its people a certain narrowness of pride, and it was in their pride, perhaps, that they were vulnerable. In the swift and often chaotic change of the world about them they liked to assure themselves that in their own corner of that world, spiritual and cultural values still transcended the material, and they clung tightly to the precious remnants of their way of life to prevent its being absorbed and lost in the mainstream.

Sometimes when Megan Casey stood at her window looking down at the town she was reminded, in ways, of the eastern village where she had grown up, save that it was somewhat larger. Almost anyplace, she thought wryly, was somewhat larger than her hometown.

Occasionally she felt a nostalgic twinge for that other town, the place of her birth which lay nearly a continent away. Although at eighteen she had been anxious to escape, she had known a good childhood there. Her parents' home had been a sprawling, shabbily comfortable frame house on an acreage just outside the city limits. Her father was the village druggist, but he grew garden truck and kept horses and a cow, and a barnyard flock. It helped satisfy his Irish love of the land.

Her parents' marriage had been a genuinely good one. Casey had never seen them display much open affection—how was it, then, that she had always known how deeply they loved each other? By a look exchanged, a small secret smile—whatever, she had known.

If I could have a marriage like theirs, I'd buy, but I don't think they're making that kind anymore.

I've been a disappointment to them.

She thought it with a kind of detachment. What they would have liked would have been for her to follow in the footsteps of her sister, Annie. Annie, fifteen years Casey's senior, graduated high, went to business college, and married Lee Milton, the son of the town banker. Annie and Lee had it made. In time, when his father retired, Lee would in turn become the town banker. They had a split-level ranch-house-type home, a social life full of country-club golf and dinners and bridge, and their kids—two of them to date—would have the best of everything. And Casey would not have traded places with them for anything in the world.

It was largely Lee and Annie who had seen Casey through State University, and she should be grateful to them. She was grateful, but she was spared any envy of them, not for their affluence, or their apparent marital contentment. What they had was not what it would take to satisfy Casey. Of course, were Casey asked what it would take to satisfy her, she was not certain what to reply. Not happiness, she knew that for what it was, an ephemeral sometime thing. Excitement? Enough, at any rate, to keep from being bored, because boredom was a thing she coped badly with. Reality, certainly—no pretty window-dressing kind of life which made its daily bow to the conventions and was, in fact, dull as hell.

Maybe if she had gotten off to a different start, she might have settled for the sort of life Annie and Lee had. She was certain Lee was the only man Annie had ever slept with. The girls with whom Casey had grown up had a different set of values. None of them had ever heard of the pill, but more than a majority of them carried contraceptives in their purses; and the *in* thing for junior and senior girls was to have a boyfriend with whom one went steady, with all that denoted. Casey had her own boyfriend, one Rick Toland. She'd been crazy about him. A lot of the girls eventually married their steadies, some of them shotgun weddings, some not. In the back of Casey's mind she had assumed she and Rick would marry, one day. When she felt a nagging guilt because of her parents' implicit and misplaced trust in her, she forgave herself by saying to herself that after all, she and Rick truly loved each other.

Their true love had lasted throughout her junior and his senior year and the summer vacation. In the fall, Rick went away to college, vowing his eternal constancy. It was a short eternity, with Rick's letters, his ardor when he saw Casey during brief holidays, gradually waning. Casey's pride had obliged her to break off with him, and Rick had made only a token protest. For a time she had been heartbroken and fiercely determined never to love another man as long as she lived. With time her heart had healed, and she realized that marriage to Rick Toland was not what she really wanted. By then she was certain that marriage itself was not what she really wanted.

Measured by her family's standards, she knew, she was an oddball. Her mother could not understand why she wanted to work so far from home, getting back maybe once or twice a year. "It isn't like you'd married some man whose work took him off somewhere; that I could understand. A woman has to go where her man goes. But chasing off by yourself—"

Casey's father came a bit nearer to understanding. "You're like your Aunt Meg." This was the relative for whom Casey had been named—Megan, the aunt who had lived in Ireland, single to the day of her death, and a bit of a wanderer. "Always on the go, she was, wanting to do the things she'd never done, see the places she'd never seen—a kind of restless wanting. I expect you come by it honest."

Well, there were places Casey had seen now, although not so many yet; and there were things she'd done—too many, maybe. Her life would be a shocking thing to mamma, X-rated. Nice Girls did not sleep with men they had no intention of marrying. Nice Girls, in fact, married the men before they slept with them at all. There was no way Casey could have explained to her that simply because one chose not to commit herself fully and forever to one man, it did not follow that she must take a vow of chastity.

A trifle impatiently she put mamma, and home, out of her mind. A flash of color from the open space on a rise above the college campus caught her eye. The Tarant football squad was out for early scrimmage, their jerseys brightly red in the October morning sunlight.

She smiled, recalling Ted Dunlap's quip, "Tarant never had a team until just a few years ago. In fact, you could say Tarant has never yet had a football team." Ted was the college athletic director, big, good-looking, unmarried. He had more than a passing thing for Casey, whom he called Megan.

"I don't like this business of last names for women. It desexes them."

Casey had wondered vaguely whether that was a chauvinistic attitude she should resent, and decided that on the contrary she rather liked it.

Ted was a darned attractive guy, and definitely the marrying kind. She thought it possible she might have gone for him, had she not been carrying the torch for Jeff Kendall. Besides his physical attractiveness, Ted had a nice sense of humor, and a deep-seated respect for women. The latter, she thought, might well be on its way to becoming a trait extinct among American males. Some time ago she had left off vowing that she would never marry; and when it came right down to it, Ted Dunlap was husband material. Jeff Kendall was definitely not.

Ted knew about Casey and Jeff, but whatever he felt of disapproval he kept to himself. Casey liked him, enjoyed his company, and she dated him occasionally. It threw the campus gossips off stride. He was a good friend, and although she was aware he would have liked to be more than that to her, he did not push, save that now and then he referred to himself, wryly, as Casey's trained red herring.

He laughed at Tarant, with its antiquities. The town, he said, had a no-growth policy, wanting things to remain unchanged. For many years the college, which was the town's focal point, its reason for being, had not been obliged to change if it chose not to, being privately endowed. In more recent years, however, it had become necessary to seek public funding, and with that capitulation inevitable change had set in. It was true the future-shock wave had not yet fully rolled over the place and in some ways Casey considered it rather a pity that it must. Tarant was an intriguing museum piece and perhaps it really should be preserved for future generations to marvel at.

Sometimes during her first months there she had asked herself, "What's a bad girl like you doing in a nice place like this?"

It was simple, really. She had fled a position with a city advertising agency. Well, actually what she had fled from was a love affair which was going sour, with the man pressing for more of herself and her life than she was willing to give. In a trade journal she picked up in her office one day, there had been this ad for an executive secretary in a place called Tarant College. She had looked up the town of Tarant on a map. It was in the boonies, on the edge of the mountains, on the edge of civilization. On an impulse she boarded a plane and flew in for an interview—and here she was.

When she chose to live in an apartment in town the dean of women, one Margaret Adkins, made it clear she preferred all unmarried personnel to reside on campus. Casey made a perfunctory inspection of the cramped, outmoded women's dormitories, and said a quick thank you, but no, thank you. She made it clear in turn that she had been on her own for nearly ten years, and preferred to make her own decisions as to where she would quarter.

"We do," said Miss Adkins, "like to feel that our people will be aware of their responsibility to set a good example for the young students," and Casey repressed a grin, to smile sweetly instead.

"Most of what I know, good and bad, I learned in school myself. These kids have had several years to get one up on me, but I promise to be very circumspect. All right?"

"All right." Miss Adkins permitted herself a small smile in reply, albeit a wintery one. "At least, we'll see, won't we?"

Casey had been as good as her word with Miss Adkins during that first year. She was so circumspect that she nearly perished of boredom during the hours when she was not actually working. It was not from choice, but she was selective and there was no man to whom she was attracted. Correction, there had been one after a time, but he had taken his own sweet leisure becoming aware of Megan Casey. She had often thought that if she had been acquainted with Ted Dunlap then the course of events might have been greatly altered.

When she moved from the president's office to the position of secretary to Doctor Jeffrey Kendall and general factotum to the entire psychology department—a move not unattended by some plain and fancy maneuvering on her part—Jeff had shown little interest in where she lived, or how, or if. It was months before he seemed aware that she lived at all save in orderly manuscripts, pages of tabulated figures, neatly typed letters, and reports which she placed on his desk.

There were times when she sensed that in some dark area within himself Jeff Kendall was a troubled man, but she said firmly that, for the most part, if ever she had known a human who had his life all together, that one was Jeff Kendall. Beneath his offhand manner was a genuinely concerned human being. He was sensitive to the needs of his students, enormously popular with them. Often Casey monitored his lectures through the open doorway of her office which adjoined the classroom. She was intrigued by the way he involved his students in confrontations with themselves and each other; and she had listened with amusement to an assignment he gave which caused a flurry among them.

"I want each of you to run a personal inventory on yourself. What do you like most about you? Dislike the most? Try to be as objective as possible. View yourself as someone else might."

A girl's voice demanded pertly, "What you mean is would I want myself as my best friend, right?" and the class laughed. Jeff laughed, too.

"Something like that. Presumably you are in this course because you want to learn how the human animal functions, mentally and emotionally. To even approach that sort of understanding, you need to learn to understand yourselves, insofar as possible."

"Do we have to write it out, this inventory thing?"

"That's the general idea. Set it down in black and white, as honestly as you can, with no temporizing, no rationalizing."

"And we have to turn this in to you?"

"Would that bother you?"

"Well, how do I know until I write it? I might not want anyone to see it."

"Hey," a boy's voice broke in, "that's the whole thing, isn't it? I mean, you know, showing it to someone else, you'd have to level. Like another guy would be able to tell if you were faking it. That's neat!"

"What I'm hoping is that some of you will be willing to share your self-evaluations with the group. I won't make sharing it mandatory. Just try it, and we'll see how it plays."

"Let me know how it plays," Casey told him, later. "That was some chore you laid on those kids. Have you ever tried it?"

"That," Jeff rejoined with a grin, "is none of your business. Would you like to try it?"

"Forget it. I'm not one of your students—anyway, the things I'm learning from you aren't being taught in the classroom, yet. I consider me charming, intelligent, unselfish and sexy. Why should I expose me to a bunch of characters who might just tell me it ain't necessarily so?"

She knew Jeff's concern for the young was real, and it manifested itself in larger ways in his off-campus activities, which were viewed by some of his colleagues with attitudes ranging from misgiving to outright disapproval. He was on the board of directors, in an advisory capacity, of a down-county group known as Turnaround, a rehabilitation house for teenagers with alcohol- and drug-abuse problems. He had also aided in establishing a telephone "hotline" and devised a training program for personnel to handle calls from despairing people: would-be suicides, runaways, alcoholics, addicts, the lonely, the abandoned.

Casey chafed at the criticism leveled at him by those who felt such activities demeaned Tarant's image as a theologically oriented school. The biggest flap came when Jeff arbitrarily inaugurated, in his department, a comprehensive course in alcoholic counseling. When the regents, backed by a group of Jeff's peers, confronted him with their disapproval, he let go an angry blast at them.

"I'm hanged if I can understand how your minds work. Here you have a seminary which grinds out young ministers all set to go into the world and tell other people how to live. That's great if they have a congregation full of saints who don't need help, but if they're going to minister to the needy, then there are things they must know. For instance, that you can rarely save a drunk or an addict by preaching at him or praying over him, and that goes for a lot of other human illnesses you people diagnose as *sin*. If I had my way you wouldn't graduate a single man from that preacher factory of yours until he'd had intensive courses in all kinds of counseling."

The old guard were infuriated at Jeff's plain, sometimes brutal way of expressing his views, but thus far he had usually won out. That he was an asset to the school even his warmest enemies could not deny. He was becoming increasingly well known through his work and his writing. Students sought out his courses. There were other schools which wanted him. Sooner or later he might go over to one of them, and doubtless colleagues like Rolfe Amboy hoped it might be sooner.

The time had come when Casey dared to say, "There are so many contradictory sides to you that understanding you is like trying to dope out one of those instant-insanity puzzles. Psychologists make a career from figuring out what makes humanity jibe, don't they? Did anyone ever try to figure out how a psychologist is put together?"

"I suspect we get interested in trying to unriddle our own hang-ups and when we botch that we move on to being expert at fixing up other people's."

"And what is your greatest hang-up?"

"I thought I just told you. *I* am."

Eventually, of course, the endearing little things about Jeff got the better of her judgment, she found herself thinking too often about the way his face lighted when he smiled, his quick and often wild sense of humor. Somewhere along the line she fell in love, for the first time in her life.

It did not bother her at first that he was not marriage minded. Neither was she. There had been other affairs for Jeff, she knew that. He was a sensual man, attractive to women and attracted by them. Still, they would not have been cheap dalliances for mere physical gratification, but real friendships to which he would have brought all his warmth and charm and innate decency.

There had been others for Casey; Jeff knew, and it didn't matter to him. When her own feelings began to get more complicated, that was small comfort to her. Maybe, she thought, it was simple that *she* didn't matter that much to him.

Ours isn't a love affair, it's one of those meaningful relationships; gay, warm, comforting, comfortable—expendable.

One or two of the men she had known had been willing to bestow upon her their name, a suburban mortgage, kids if she wanted them. She had sent them on their way. It was as if she had been waiting—for what? Waiting for a Jeff Kendall was like waiting for a ship which had already sailed. Sometimes her mind twiddled wearily with words which had greatly appealed to her a few years ago—modern, emancipated, free.

The new morality? The hell with it! If I had the last few years to live over I'd live them differently, just in case the kind of guy I'd like to shack up with for keeps isn't quite ready for my kind of freedom.

Her affair with Jeff had begun quite abruptly on a winter night two years ago when he returned from Canada and the funeral of his father. He was tired and dispirited, and when he came to Casey for quiet talk and companionship, it ended with her holding him close, making solacing sounds. That night she had learned— women's lib, please copy and never mind if the lesson came a trifle late—that she threw back definitely and irreversibly to generations of women who believed their most precious privilege was to aid and comfort their men.

It hurt her that in the wan, impersonal light of morning Jeff was regretful.

"What can I say to you—that I'm sorry?"

Sorry for what? That he had taken advantage of her sympathy? She was no virginal child whom he had deflowered. That he had involved himself with her and possibly damaged a valued employer-employee relationship?

"I'm a big girl, capable of taking full responsibility for my own behavior. If I hadn't wanted it to happen it wouldn't have happened. It's that simple."

"You're a wonderful girl."

Tha banality of it outraged her. "Rubbish—and if you dare tell me how fond you are of me, I'll stick my head out the window and holler rape!"

Why hadn't she left him then? He had offered to let her go. She knew he was not in love with her. She was lovely and intelligent and warm, he said, and she had much to offer. Under the circumstances, if she stayed now he was human enough to want—Well, you understand.

Jeff had said a lot of things but not, of course, I love you. Never in all the times which followed, I love you. She told herself she would not have wanted him to say it unless he meant it.

The rules he played by had been her rules, too. So don't try to change the game now. If you can't take the heat, get out of the kitchen.

In her desire to hold him she put down his first doubts lightly. "Don't go all twaddly on me, Jeff. We're both lonely, and let's face it, in this rarified academic atmosphere we could both do worse."

Inside her she shed the same tears females in love have shed ever since the globe was set spinning. She indulged in fantasies of his coming to her to say wonderingly, I love you, I think I've loved you from the beginning—

And performing in the center ring, ladies and gentlemen, Miss Megan Casey and her trained love. It will roll over and play dead, it will sit up and beg. . . .

Like hell it will! It will take what it can get and run with it, and when the party's over don't sing me no sad songs, friend.

A rather plain woman, Helene had said.

Casey studied her own reflection in the mirror. She saw a tall girl with dusky hair and alert dark eyes. She had a long-legged, handsomely made body and her face had the ineffable combination of bones and planes which imparts a certain mystery. An artist she met at a party once explained about the bones and planes. Translated, it meant he thought she might be an exciting piece of sex and he was eager to explore the matter. He was witty and amusing, and she had gone out with him several times. She had not gone to bed with him. Not all her relationships had ended as *relationships*.

A married woman, Helene had said.

That was bad. There were things even Jeff Kendall couldn't get away with in a backwater like Tarant, where there were too many people itching to pull him down.

Jeff had an uncle, a priest, who was living up at Shadow Lake in the mountains, recuperating from a lengthy illness. He and Casey had come to be friends. He liked having her call, if only so he could chide her for the fact that although she was Irish Catholic by birth, she was nothing much at all by inclination. Casey was tempted to call, or even to drive up there for a visit; she had done that on occasion when she felt the urge to get away from Tarant for a little while. Maybe through Father Francis she could get at the truth of what was going on.

Pride prevented her. Even if he knows about Jeff and this Shane, what makes you think he'd tell you? He might think, and rightly so, that if Jeff wants you to know he can bloody well tell you himself, right?

She would simply have to play it by ear. With any luck, what's-her-name would soon be winging her way back to home and husband.

Tomorrow Jeff will be here and you'll have your turn at bat, so just cool it!

Her telephone was ringing again. When she answered, a girl's voice said, "Casey? This is Maryanne Anderson. I've got to get in touch with Doctor Kendall and I was wondering—well, I mean, it's really a kind of emergency and I thought maybe you can tell me when he'll be back in his office."

Casey hesitated. Maryanne was one of Jeff's brightest students, a pretty kid with a high IQ. At first she had posed something of a personal problem for him, because she had had a terrific crush on him and for several hectic weeks she had nearly driven the poor guy up the wall with her dogged pursuit. However, she was involved with a steady boyfriend now, and recently Jeff had mentioned that he was working toward getting her qualified to take a special scholarship test down at State.

She asked, cautiously, "Has this—emergency anything to do with your schoolwork, Maryanne?"

"Yes, it has, in a way." Then she gave a nervous little giggle. "Oh, don't worry, Casey, I'm not setting a trap for him. That's a dead issue, didn't you know?"

"We-ll, he's terribly busy just now, and I'm not sure how much time he could spare you even if you catch him—but he did call me, a few moments ago. He's going to be out of town again, but he may not have left his office yet. You might try there."

"Thanks, Casey. I really *need* to talk to him, right away."

She hung up and Casey thought gloomily, That makes two of us, baby. Lots of luck!

2.
(Jeff)

He parked his car at the curb in front of Schuler Hall and walked across the quadrangle, feeling the autumn nip of night air as yet unwarmed by the early sun. Somewhere nearby some early-bird citizen was burning leaves and the sharp not-unpleasant aroma hung in the still air.

The campus was very quiet, although he could hear the faint clatter of trash-bin lids as some custodian went about his morning tasks. Lang Hall, too, was deserted and his footsteps rang hollowly on the hallway floor as he went along it to his office.

He took papers from his briefcase, clipped them together with a hastily scribbled note, *Three copies, please,* and put them on Casey's desk. He hesitated briefly, then beneath the directive he sketched a grinning face and scrawled below it *Have a good day!*

When he telephoned Casey this morning she had not been in a good mood. He could hardly fault her for that, considering the hour; still her attitude rang, as it occasionally did of late, a small warning bell in the back of his mind. Was she developing a proprietary tendency, or was that only in his imagination?

What he had with Casey was a complete understanding, at least it had been in the beginning and he hoped it still was. Both of them were aware that long-range affairs had a built-in hazard, they could become a habit no longer really desirable but difficult to break, threatening a permanency neither of them really wanted.

His own mood, he conceded, was not all that good. He disliked emotional problems which lay beyond his power—or even his right—to solve. The ending of his brief affair with Shane Manning disturbed him. He had always liked to consider himself a fairly mature, aware individual, cognizant of his inclinations and weaknesses, and in control of them. His feelings now were difficult to decipher. He had been under the clear impression that Shane's marriage was on the rocks, although in retrospect he was obliged to acknowledge that she had never said so in so many words. They had talked about many things, but never about her personal life. He sensed that she was a very private person, and he had respected her privacy. He had sensed, too, that there was an odd sort of deliberation with which she allowed herself to become emotionally and physically involved with him, as if in outright defiance of some moral code of her own.

The lady, he decided ruefully, was a puzzlement. He had never known a woman like her. Of course, he had never had an affair with a married woman before, and that, obviously, had its own built-in hazards. Now she was ending the affair herself, going back to her husband, and Jeff Kendall was going back to—what?

Here was the most disturbing factor of all, maybe—that the idea of taking up where he had left off with Casey held no appeal. It was not that he no longer cared for her. Casey was some kind of lady, warm and desirable, with a mental sharpness which made her a delightful companion. He felt precisely the same about her as he had always felt—and there was the rub. In the beginning of their relationship there had been tacit agreement that if either of them reached the point at which he now stood, he or she had only to say the word to write *finis* to the affair, with no regrets and no recriminations. It would be a hell of a lot simpler, though, if both of them could have arrived at that point at the same time. His friendship with Casey had meant a great deal to him and he did not want to hurt her. It did small good to remind himself that the relationship was now ending the way both of them had known that it must. He did not want to consider the possibility that Casey was involved beyond the point of no return.

He went to his desk and sat down, looking at a bunch of student papers Casey had stacked neatly there to await his attention. Maybe he'd work for a while. He had been with Shane until well after midnight. She'd probably be sleeping late this morning and then she would have things to do to get ready for her departure. He could hardly impose himself on her before midafternoon. The idea of spending the intervening hours in the company of Uncle Francis did not appeal. One of the doubtful joys of having for an uncle a priest to whom one was rather close was that it was somewhat like having a second conscience, a moral alarm clock at your elbow, set to go off at unlikely hours.

He shrugged off his thoughts and picked up a paper from the stack. It had a name scrawled untidily on it. Randy Bedaker. Looking at it, Jeff grinned reminiscently. Good kid, Bedaker, with a mind of his own. He'd gotten himself into trouble with the school authorities for leading a protest against compulsory chapel attendance. At least he had tried to lead it, although the thing never really got off the ground because Tarant students were not protest oriented and did not know how to bring it off effectively; but from the flap it caused one would have thought the kid was heading up a plot to bomb the administration building.

Jeff had gone to bat for him, facing down an outraged administrative committee and a couple of regents who had gotten into the act. Rolfe Amboy, never slow to oppose Jeff when the opportunity presented itself, had his lengthy say, and the whole thing had ended up in a kind of shouting match between the two of them.

"It's the trouble with the youth today, they make a fetish of rebelling against authority. We've never had that sort of thing at Tarant, and I for one do not propose that we countenance it now."

Jeff asked, "Have you ever wondered exactly why they rebel?" and Rolfe smiled thinly.

"If you feel you know, Doctor Kendall, please enlighten us."

"For one thing, they see authority simply for authority's sake as a put-down. Our fathers were raised up believing that at a certain point in adulthood there comes an emotional and moral stability which makes the adult infallible, capable of keeping things all neat and fail-safe. You and I know that isn't necessarily true, and the kids know it. We've generated the need for great men, but we are failing to generate the greatness—and they know that, too. Now the time has passed when you can say to them, 'You will do this' or 'You will do that' simply because it is the rule. They want a better reason than that."

Rolfe Amboy gazed into space and asked of no one in particular, "Does Doctor Kendall believe, then, that we are relieved of our duty to teach these young people the difference between right and wrong?"

Jeff snorted. "Doctor Kendall doesn't believe that was ever our primary duty. We're here to teach them to *think*, to make decisions for themselves. We're talking in generalities now. Let's bring it closer to home. If your intent is to turn these kids off, insure that they'll never walk through a church door again once they aren't forced to—fine. You couldn't settle on a more foolproof way."

He had the disgusted feeling he was wasting his breath. Of all the thousands of men and women who made a profession of teaching young minds to *cope*, he thought the faculty at Tarant, for the most part, must come at the foot of the list. They were living in a lost generation, applying a Christian Science kind of logic to cold, unpalatable facts by declining to acknowledge them; assuring themselves that nothing fundamental had changed and with time, and firm authority, the young people in their care must inevitably come around to a safe and sane way of thinking. *Their* way.

Young Bedaker had drawn a suspension of such length that he had to work like the devil to catch up with his studies when he returned. A kid of less determination might well have tossed in the towel. In the end his ploy had worked, anyway, because when he was suspended so many students deliberately absented themselves from chapel that to suspend them all would virtually have emptied the campus. To add insult to injury, a large number of the kids managed to elicit from their parents letters supporting them in their rebellion. Ironically enough, it was a very short while after young Bedaker's suspension that the rule was rescinded, for all save seminary students.

There were footsteps outside his door and a pretty head thrust itself into view.

"Hi," said Maryanne Anderson. "Casey said I might find you here. Is it okay if I come in?"

"Come in." Jeff eyed her a bit warily. One never knew what to expect from this one. She was a study in contradictions, a bright kid, almost too bright for her own good. She was capable of talking like a little guttersnipe, behaving like an amoral wildcat, and she made the highest marks of any of his students. She was achingly aware of her sex and when she had first entered his classes, a year ago, she had made life hectic for him, pursuing him relentlessly, letting him know she was not averse to going to bed with him.

"I know it's just a girlish crush I've got on you, and I'll get over it—but until I do, why not take advantage of it?"

To be honest about it, he had been mildly flattered, and mildly tempted, if only in his fantasies. She was eighteen; by her own declaration she was no virgin. She not only had a good mind, it was beautifully packaged in a supple, sweetly curved young body. She made Jeff feel certain Mother Nature was at her wisest when she remembered to enclose the great intellects in the plainer exteriors.

He had managed to kid Maryanne out of it

without angering her or hurting her feelings. In recent months she had been going steady with young Jim Haney, a big, good-looking kid on the football squad. Haney was in Jeff's Psych II group, and he sometimes suspected most of the kid's brains were in his muscles. Privately he wished Maryanne would not waste her time on him.

At Jeff's urging, Maryanne had agreed, reluctantly, to study for some special scholarship tests scheduled at State. Even to qualify for the tests was a signal achievement, and Maryanne had done it without difficulty. She had a lot going for her, and Jeff felt her chances of making it at State were good—if she didn't cut the gun too much on a slow corner with someone like the Haney boy.

Just now, he noted that she seemed edgy and uptight. He asked sympathetically, "What's bugging you? Worried about the tests?"

She shrugged. "I'm worried, but not about the tests. I'm not going to take them."

"Maybe I didn't read that right. Do you want to run it past me again?"

"I said I'm not going to take the tests." She faced him defiantly. "I'd better spell it out for you. I'm pregnant."

He let out his breath in a sigh. "Officially?"

"I got my report from the clinic a week ago. It's official."

"Am I correct in assuming it's young Haney's child?"

"Of course you're correct!" Her temper flared. "Who else's would it be? I'm just a tramp, not a whore."

"Steady on." He smiled at her. "If you're going to feel sorry for yourself, then it saves me the trouble of being sorry for you, right? So what now?"

"I'm going to have the kid, if that's what you mean."

"I didn't mean anything in particular. I was simply asking a question."

"This baby is going to get born. I've read the articles and listened to the talk about abortion. If the experts can't agree on when a—when it gets to be a *person*, then I don't feel like taking the chance. I mean, if it's a human being already, then it has the right to a life of its own. Afterward, I don't know if I would keep it or give it away. That's a decision I'll have to make when the time comes."

"Does Haney know?"

"He knows." She gave Jeff a flickering grin. "He and I don't agree on what he ought to do about it. He wants to get married."

"And you don't?"

"I don't, and I won't. Fun is one thing," her chin lifted defiantly, "but marrying him is something else."

"What about your parents?"

"My dad would kill me—not that he's anyone to point the finger. He and my mom have been married for twenty-two years and they've hated each other for at least twenty of that. Dad plays around and she knows it. I don't think she cares. It keeps him out of her bed. She thinks sex is dirty. Hell! Why am I wasting time talking about them? They don't count—I'm for damned sure not going home."

"Well, now. You're going to have a baby. You don't want to get married and you don't want to go home. What do you want? You'll have to have help from somewhere."

"I don't know." She studied him for a moment and then gave a little laugh. "You shouldn't have turned me down. With you, this would never have happened."

He ignored that. "How long will you be able to stay in school?"

"I'm a little over two months along. I can probably make it to the end of the semester before I get to showing so much they'll kick me out."

"You know that's precisely what they'll do, don't you?" he queried, and she nodded, shrugging. "Well, the first thing is to be very certain just how *you* feel, and obviously you've been doing some serious thinking about that. It's important for you to make the decision you can live most comfortably with, afterward."

"That's how I see it. I know what my folks would say—mom would be shocked and disgusted because I'd let some boy do nasty things with me. Dad would say get rid of it—he'd keep at me and at me until maybe I'd give in and do what he wanted, just to get him off my back." She shook her head. "Maybe it's just a . . . a *nothing* now, but I'd never really be sure, would I?" Jeff realized that suddenly she was trying not to cry. Her air of bravado was deserting her. "I'm scared, really scared—you know?"

"I think so, but it isn't going to help matters any to blow your cool. Most problems have a solution. We'll have to find it, that's all." He felt the need to divert her thoughts for the moment, and he asked, "Tell me, how did you happen to choose Tarant College?"

Maryanne shrugged. "This was my father's hometown. He grew up here."

"He was a student at Tarant?"

"No, he never went here, but my grandmother lived here until she died. When I was a little kid I used to spend most of my summers here. I was crazy about Gram. She was really something, that lady. I don't know how she had a son like my father, I mean some of the things he does, it must have bugged her, if she knew. She was kind of old-fashioned. She used to make me go to Sunday school every week, but it was okay, you know? Like I really grooved on it, all that stuff about how gentle and kind Jesus was and how He wanted everyone to be good. I used to think when I grew up I was going to be something special, just for Him, like maybe a missionary." Her little laugh was touched with sadness. "But when I was fourteen, something happened that really turned me off. I had a brother, Kevin. He was two years older, and we weren't really close, but I liked him a lot. When he was a senior in high school he took to running with a really wild crowd and he got started using. He fought with my parents a lot, and it was pretty gross. I knew something heavy was going down, but I didn't understand much of it. I was kind of dumb for a kid my age, I guess. Anyway, one night Kevin was at a party and he OD'd. It killed him." She took a restless turn about the room, remembering.

Presently she said in a hard little voice, "I hated my parents then. I swear to God it was like they were more upset over what people would think about us, knowing Kevin was a doper—" She broke off with a gesture of disgust. "By then, my Gram was already dead and that was probably good. I don't think she could have handled all that crap about Kevin. But there wasn't anyone left to talk to, and it was like there wasn't any use in trying to be good, and I didn't care what I did. I've stayed away from the heavy stuff but I've smoked pot plenty of times, and as far as that goes, I've done just about everything else I've felt big enough to handle. I don't know why; I never really enjoyed any of it. Sometimes I told myself I was living for myself and Kevin, too, you know? I wanted to experience everything he was missing out on. That was a kind of cop-out, though—even if I kept the things I was doing from my folks, I didn't really give a damn if they found out. Maybe I wanted them to, to punish them for Kevin. Oh, I'm sure they loved him, but I think just loving isn't enough if it isn't the right kind." She turned to look at Jeff with a challenging quality in her stare. "I guess you think I'm talking shit."

"No, I think you're telling it as you feel it."

"I've done a lot of yakking to get around to why I came here. Gram and I had made it up between us that when I was ready for college I'd come here and stay with her, for the first two years, at least. When I graduated from high school I decided to do it anyway. I'm not sure why—for Gram, maybe. She was the only person I ever knew that I really wanted to please. I knew I'd started doing a lot of things that would have broken her heart, and it was like this was one thing I could do that she'd wanted me to. I'd always been a good student and she was real proud of that—" Then, with abrupt change of topic:

"Do you think I'm wrong, not wanting to marry Jim?"

"I think you're the only person who could decide that. Certainly I can't. I'm sure you have your reasons for not wanting to marry him."

"Well, for openers, I don't love him. I don't even like him all that much anymore. He's just a kid himself and he wouldn't have the least idea how to go about being a husband or father. It wouldn't be fair to expect it of him; it just wouldn't work. Is it so important to give a baby a name, if it means you have to give it the wrong kind of father?" She moved restlessly about, went to a window to stare out. "God, I don't know why I ever got in so deep with him. At first, I really grooved on him, you know? But then I began to see how infantile he is in some ways. He was jealous and possessive, like a little kid. It got to be a really bad scene and I should have split only—would you believe me if I said the real reason I didn't—I didn't want to hurt him?"

"I'd believe you."

"It's really wild. I mean, Jim was a *virgin*, can you dig it? God!" She made a self-deprecatory little sound. "I felt like two cents when I figured that one out. Sure, he was going to start laying girls sometime, but I wasn't all that proud of being the one to break him in. Look, I'm a smart-ass, I know it. I don't like myself for it, but I guess I don't know how to be any other way. I wish to God I knew what living is all about—I don't even know what *I'm* all about. But I don't like hurting people. Now I suppose I'll be hurting Jim worse than if I had quit him a long time ago. He says if I want to—to get rid of it—he'll get the money from his folks, some way, but I won't do that and I can't marry him." She struck a small fist against the windowsill. "I just don't *know!*"

"There's not much point in second-guessing what's already been done. The important thing is to try to get some sense of direction from here. I think it's good, your planning to stay in school as long as you can, but you do need to know where you'll go when you can't stay here any longer."

"There are places—homes for unwed mothers." She gave it a wry sound. "I don't know what they cost, or anything. I won't go to one where it's part of the arrangement that you agree to put the baby up for adoption. I want to make up my own mind about that when it's born. Gram left me a little money. I was supposed to get it when

I turned eighteen but my father talked me into letting it alone until I got out of school. Anyway, the money is mine and I can get it whenever I want. What I mean is, I don't have to go to a charity place—you know, like welfare, or that. If it isn't too much, I can pay my own way."

"All right, let me do some checking. I have friends who would know. I'll get all the information, procedures, costs, the whole ball of wax. Meanwhile, you'll want to provide yourself with good prenatal care, to safeguard your health, and the child's."

"I've already thought about that. I haven't thought about much of anything else, lately. You know something? It's corny, but I wish to God I'd been good, like Gram wanted me to be." She was near tears again and with a surge of pity he recognized the youthful agony in her. "If I was going to raise a kid I'd want to teach it to be good. End of joke. Laugh here."

"What does that mean?"

"If you're bad yourself, how do you go about teaching someone else to be good?"

"Doing what you call bad things doesn't necessarily mean you're a bad person. The real cop-out would be to write everything off with the excuse that you're bad and there's no use trying to be anything else. You can be whatever you want to be. The trick is to want it badly enough to be willing to do something about it. Do you know what you want?"

She shrugged. "I guess I don't. I only know I want my life to mean something; I don't want to just put in my time. I know you were trying to help me with the scholarship business and I was a fool to screw it up, but I did, and that's that."

"Not necessarily. You know, you haven't the right to try to punish someone else for his faults, and it's foolish to attempt to punish yourself for your own. Look, I have an idea you can try on for size. Go ahead and take the tests. If you make out, we'll see what can be done about a deferred scholarship. Let's not start burning bridges, okay?"

For the moment she gazed uncertainly at him, then she said in a subdued voice, "Sure, I guess so. Okay."

"Good. We'll take it one step at a time."

She drew a deep breath. "*Wow*. I got up this morning feeling like the whole world was coming right down around my ears. Thanks for not preaching at me."

"Did you think I might?"

"I wasn't sure, but I knew whatever you did, you wouldn't hand me a bunch of bullshit. I know I must have been pretty much of a pain to you sometimes, and I'm sorry about that, I really am. I guess I just wanted you to notice me."

Jeff rejoined, dryly, "I noticed you."

"Yeah. Well, I must have made an awful fool of myself. Jim said I did—in fact, that's how I first came to notice *him*, because one day before class he made a snotty remark about my chasing after you." She was laughing a little, now. "You know, you're really some kind of very special guy."

"What I am is some kind of very busy guy who's going to chase you out right now so I can get some work done." He left his desk and crossed over to her, to take her hand and lead her gently but firmly toward the door. "You try not to worry too much, and above all, don't go off on any crazy tangents. I'll get back to you as soon as I have some information for you. Meanwhile, see if you can relax enough to get your mind on those tests. Deal?"

"Deal." She looked up at him. "What can I say? Just 'thank you' seems so *dumb*."

"It'll do." He was a little embarrassed by the gratitude shining in her eyes. "Go on, now, beat it!"

Now he was in no mood for work and he left the building himself a few moments later. He saw Ted Dunlap's battered station wagon parked outside the student union and on an impulse he crossed over and went in. The athletic director was sitting alone at a table, eating breakfast. Jeff got himself a cup of coffee and went over, to say, " 'Morning, Dunlap, mind if I join you?" and as the other glanced up, nodding assent, he slid into the chair opposite.

The two of them knew each other only casually, although Jeff supposed some might say they had something in common. Dunlap was a decent sort, and Jeff liked him.

"I wanted to ask your opinion of something—of someone, rather." He paused, and Dunlap waited, his regard politely curious. "You know the Haney boy rather well, I'd imagine, Jim Haney?"

"He's on the squad, and the track team. I see considerable of him." He made it a flat statement and waited again. Jeff nodded.

"Would you care to tell me something about him, what sort of kid he is?"

Dunlap countered, "Would you care to tell me why you want to know?" and Jeff grinned.

"Matter of fact, I wouldn't care to. I have a reason, however. It isn't just idle curiosity."

"You have him in one of your classes, haven't you? I seem to recall your giving him a conditional flunk last semester. It knocked him out of the regional track meet. We lost."

"Would you have won it with him?"

Dunlap grinned, too. "Probably not. The other schools were better than we were. . . . Maryanne

Anderson is a student of yours, too, isn't she?"

"Yes, she is. Why do you ask?"

Dunlap set his coffee cup down and folded his arms. "Maybe we shouldn't play *I've Got a Secret*. Yes, I know Haney pretty well. He talks to me quite a bit." His glance measured Jeff. "And I saw Maryanne coming out of your building as I came in to breakfast. There aren't many people she'd be going to see in Lang Hall at that hour—and your car was at the curb. Anyway, she told Jim she was going to talk to you."

"You know about it, then."

"Yes." He picked up his fork and drew an invisible design on the tabletop, scowling at it. "It's a tough break for both of them. Jim is scared out of his wits."

"Maryanne tells me he's willing to do the right thing by her."

"Did she also tell you she won't have any part of it?"

"Yes. I think she means it."

"I think she does, too. It's too bad, maybe— it's probably the only way they could both manage to stay in school, once this thing gets around."

"Well, I have no intention of offering her any advice with regard to that, but I was curious to know what you think of Haney. I only have him in the one class and that's hardly a fair premise on which to make an appraisal."

"But your impression of him is that he's a lightweight."

"I didn't say that."

"No, you didn't, but if it is your impression, I'd have to tell you that in my opinion you're right. Jim's a nice enough kid and I like him, but frankly he isn't in the girl's class now, and I'd venture to guess she'll outdistance him even more as time goes by—always provided, of course, that she doesn't go straight to hell in a hand basket first. For my money, it could go either way. She's as wild as they come."

"Oh, I don't know. I think she's fundamentally pretty sound. She is determined to have the child and while I wouldn't care to conjecture as to the wisdom of that, it does say something for her, in my opinion. She seems to feel she couldn't expect any sympathy or understanding from her people."

"I suppose this blows her chances for the scholarship."

"Not necessarily. I'm encouraging her to go ahead with the tests. If she makes the grade, then we'll see what can be done about getting the scholarship deferred. I know a couple of people at State who can probably help, if I explain the situation to them. Fortunately, they march to a slightly different kind of music than we do here at Tarant."

Dunlap nodded. "Almost anyplace does. Still, it's a mess—she'll be washed up here when the word gets out, and I'd say Jim can expect the same."

"That rather depends. I'm sure Maryanne wouldn't involve him, given a choice. She's too independent for that."

"They'll hardly need proof. Have you never heard of the 'very appearance of evil?' I'll lay you dollars to doughnuts they find some excuse for booting him out. I'm not saying it's any fairer for her to have to leave than for him. Unfortunately, she's the one who'll be carrying the physical evidence."

"True."

"I feel sorry for the girl. Of course, she's of legal age, so if she doesn't want to go home, she can't be forced to. It's too bad she doesn't have some woman she can talk to. I can imagine how much sympathy and understanding she'd get from Margaret Adkins."

That brought a laugh from Jeff. The Tarant dean of women was a fiftyish spinster, and a virgin to boot, he'd make book on it. Then he said thoughtfully, "You know, that is an idea. I don't suppose she and Casey know each other well, but Casey has a good head on her shoulders, and she might be a great deal of help, if Maryanne will let her."

A sudden awkward little silence fell, then Dunlap said, "Listen, I've got kids working out at the field, and I'd better get back. If I can help in any way—"

"Right. We'll keep in touch." Jeff sat for a moment, watching the other man walk away. Dunlap had tightened up perceptibly at the mention of Casey's name. It irritated Jeff.

All right, damn it, I have something he wants. Even if I should no longer want it, he can't have it, because Casey doesn't want him. That makes it Dunlap's problem, not mine.

And if Casey still wants you, that makes it her problem, right?

He arose, too, and left, striding quickly as if to outdistance the small feeling of guilt, leave it behind.

*3.
(Court)*

The red light was flashing on his desk intercom. He pushed a button and said, "Yes, Miss Hale?" and from the outer office his clerk said:

"Rod Bailey is here with the specs on the

Lambert project, Mr. Manning. He'd like to talk to you."

"Tell him to come in—no, wait, I'll come out there."

Rod Bailey was Manning Enterprises' general manager. He was a good man, but he wasted a lot of words when he had something to discuss. Let him get comfortably settled here and he'd ramble on for an hour, and Court was in no mood to listen.

He did not stir for the moment but sat looking toward the window. It had begun to rain in midmorning, steadily and soddenly, and the gathering gloom had made it necessary to have the lights on since lunchtime. It irritated him. Funny thing, he had liked rain when he was a kid, back in Tarant, but out here in sunny California a gloomy day came as an affront to the senses.

Presently he got up and went into the outer office. Bailey was leaning over Miss Hale's desk, talking to her. Looking down the front of her blouse, probably, Court thought, noting the rapt look on Bailey's face. Maybe you couldn't blame him much, at that. Miss Hale's blouse was well packed.

From where he stood, Court could see a lot of her leg. Even with miniskirts going out now, she still wore hers mighty short.

He could see the pink flesh of her inner thigh through her sheer stockings and he despised himself and her for the quickening in his loins. One of these days, he promised himself, I'm going to tell her if she wants to go on working here she'll have to put on some goddamned clothes!

Bailey straightened up quickly, looking guilty enough to let Court know he had been right.

"We're in like thieves on the Lambert job. Squires didn't quote the figures but I've a hunch we came in a good twenty thou below the nearest competitor, which was probably Atlas Electronics. Listen, I've been going over the estimates and I see where we can save ourselves a bundle by tightening up the component list on the overall amplifier system. If you'd like to take a look—"

"Not now. I'm getting ready to leave for the day. Leave the lists with me and I'll look at them tomorrow." He took the sheaf of papers Bailey held out and would have left the room, but then he stopped, the other's words only now registering. "And we won't tighten up on anything. I allowed for our full profit in the figures we submitted and that's how they stand. We don't shave quality on any job we contract for. How many times do we have to go through this, Rod?"

Bailey's face reddened. "I just thought—"

"Forget it. You know how I feel about that sort of thing."

He went into his office and closed the door. Bailey muttered between his teeth, "Up yours, too!" and Miss Hale, alarmed, reached to close a switch.

"Watch it," she said in a warning whisper, "his receiver was open."

"I don't give a damn." Bailey's face was still an angry red. "Someday—"

Miss Hale laughed at him. "Someday, nothing. You wouldn't quit Mr. Manning, and you know it. He pays good and he treats us good. So what if he happens to be honest? Can't you get used to that?"

"You gotta admit it's a little weird," Bailey said, and began to laugh, too. "Manning's a good guy; it's just that he comes on a little *too* good, sometimes."

She shook her head. "With him, it's for real."

Bailey looked appraisingly at her. "You've sorta got a thing for him, haven't you?" and laughed again when she blushed. She began a denial, then she shrugged.

"Even if I had, a fat lot of good it would do me. He doesn't know there's a woman alive but his wife."

Bailey chuckled. "Well, you gotta admit, *that's* weird!"

Court cleared his desk and moved about, turning off lights. For a moment he paused at the window, looking at the weeping sky. Manning Enterprises lay in an industrial complex of grimy buildings and presented, just now, a vista of sodden, rain-blackened roofs. Across the street in Dolly's Cafeteria he could see the busboys hustling about, putting setups on the little wooden tables. Dolly's was open twenty-four hours a day, to catch all the shifts from the surrounding plants. He had been eating over there pretty regularly in the past two months. It was good enough food, but boring as hell. He supposed when you were feeding working people on an assembly line, at economy prices, you couldn't afford to be imaginative.

He took a raincoat from the closet, shrugged into it, and put his hat on. Sometimes Bailey kidded him about the hat. "We can always tell mid-Westerners out here, they wear hats and gloves in the wintertime. The natives don't."

Bailey was a native Californian and prouder of it than Court thought he had any particular need to be. Sometimes he squelched him mildly:

"Everybody's a native son of somewhere. It's no big deal."

When he went through the outer office, Miss Hale was standing at the big filing cabinet, bent over a lower drawer, and virtually her whole backside was in plain view. Court cleared his throat and she stood up, turning around.

It was on the tip of his tongue to say, I thought short skirts were going out, Miss Hale. Why don't you sew some kind of ruffle around the bottom of that dress?

Then he thought, Oh, the hell with it.

The only reason it bothered him, her wearing those short skirts, was because it did bother him some. God knew he'd never make a pass at her, although sometimes he had the feeling she wouldn't be exactly displeased if he did.

He said, merely, "You might as well hang it up for the day, too. In this bad weather," he knew she lived out in the valley and that her home-going traffic was always heavy, "it's apt to take you a while."

"Thank you, Mr. Manning." Watching him go away, she thought about how he was really an awfully nice guy, and darned good-looking, too. He was a funny one, though. She'd worked for him for nearly three years and you'd think by now he'd be calling her by her first name. Her other bosses had, and sometimes she had called them by theirs. Not this one, though; he was Mister Manning and she was Miss Hale, and that was how that was.

In all the time she had worked here she had seen Mrs. Manning only a few times. The lady didn't come to the office often. She was kind of pretty, small and dainty looking and pleasant enough to talk to, but not at all, Miss Hale opined, the sort of person you'd expect a doll like Mr. Manning to be married to. When it came right down to it, though, she didn't know much about Mr. Manning, either. For all Manning Enterprises' employees knew of their employer and his personal life, he might just disappear into nowhere when he left the building each afternoon. At Christmastime he always gave everyone a nice bonus and extra time off, but there were no office parties; and the Mannings never invited you out to their home for a company barbecue or that, like other bosses she had had.

She knew that for several weeks now Mrs. Manning had been away somewhere, because Mr. Manning had given Miss Hale money to wire to her in some place called Tarant. And that was as much as Miss Hale knew about that.

The windshield wipers made an annoying *skiree, skiroo* sound across the wet glass. Court had to drive slowly because everyone else was. The tires made squishing sounds on the pavement and tossed up sprays of dirty water from the street. It was a bad afternoon to be driving at all unless you had to.

He progressed out of the industrial area and

along Ocean Way, past a decrepit amusement park and through an area the locals designated as Porno Park. He despised the area and would have preferred taking another route, but it was the most practical way to reach the freeway. Usually he looked straight ahead and tried not to look at the marquees, remembering with hot embarrassment the time he had actually purchased a ticket at one of the X-rated places, only to turn and walk away, tearing up the pasteboard strip and flinging it into the gutter as if it stung his fingers.

It reminded him, in turn, of another time when he had stopped in one of those topless joints and had a couple of beers. They ought to call it top-heavy, he thought disgustedly, recalling the two sleazy-looking women with bovine boobs swinging as they moved among the tables. He had thought of Shane with her slim, clean body and firm, small breasts, and beside her those broads had looked like unhealthy cows. He had left his second beer untouched and got the hell out of the place.

Sometimes he tried to analyze why he had done it. Actually, he knew what he could expect at one of those porno movies and he didn't want that crap in his mind. He was no good at analyzing his own motivation—probably what he needed was a shrink. He'd read about things like that and he could imagine the guy asking, "Do you ever fantasize?" and if he answered honestly he'd have to say, "Yes, but only about my own wife."

Sometimes he had an overwhelming fear that he might say something—dreaming, he did sometimes talk in his sleep, Shane told him—that would betray the things he felt about her, needed from her. Christ, if that ever happened he could never look her in the face again. He'd want to take a gun and blow himself away, blast his dirty mind right out of his head.

He knew Shane had been a virgin when he married her. He hadn't been. There'd been a few messy, unsatisfactory experiences with coeds, and a town girl or two. Most of the guys at Tarant fooled around some, even the seminary students. From the time he knew Shane, though, he had never really wanted any other woman, not to this very day. Then what the hell was wrong with him? How could you love a woman so much and fail so miserably at making her happy?

She had called from Tarant today, to tell him she was coming home tomorrow, and afterward he had sat at his desk for a long time, just thinking, feeling a relief that was almost a physical gut thing. There had been times since she left when he had been certain, with an emotion exquisitely balanced between understanding and unaccepting anguish, that she wasn't coming home at all. He couldn't begin to imagine life without her. Things had been rough for them in the past year or so but, at their worst, for him it was better than being without her, he knew that.

Once his fear had been so great that he had decided to make the drive back to Tarant to see her, to plead with her to give them both another chance. He'd actually put a suitcase into the car; but then he changed his mind. In their ten years of marriage Shane had usually, unquestioningly, done whatever he had wanted her to do. The decision had to be hers, now.

He had paced the floor most of that night, trying to make some sense out of the mess things were in between them. There were things he had done because he thought they were best for Shane, and they had turned out to be no good at all. Once he did a really stupid thing that was irreversible and then it was twice as bad, because she despised him for it. He despised himself, too, because he was so damned inarticulate at the very times he wanted most to tell her what it was he felt. He wanted to say he loved her more than anything in the world and if she would just tell him what it was she wanted, he would move mountains to get it for her. At the times when his anguished love and desire for her were at a fever pitch, he was cowed and shamed by her passive, uncomplaining acceptance.

Shane hadn't always been that way. Sometimes his only comfort lay in remembering how things used to be. He recalled how she had looked when he first saw her outside the registrar's office at Tarant, this girl standing alone, looking so little and vulnerable, and so pretty. He'd whistled softly and said, "Hey! That's for me!"

He was walking with a buddy, who said, "That's a no-no, friend. She's Dean Parker's niece and they do say if she brings a guy home the old boy carves him up and has him for breakfast."

Court had paid him no attention. He had a way with girls—he could say that without undue boasting—but he'd never met one who'd bowled him over at first look, the way Shane did. He'd waded right in to lay his siege without giving her a chance to send him packing, and it had worked out fine. They'd had a beautiful year together and it didn't matter a damn to him that whenever Shane's uncle saw them together, if glares had been daggers they would both have been pierced through the heart. By the time he had known Shane Parker for a month he had known he wanted to marry her, but he hadn't pushed. They'd dated and studied together and gone on picnics, all the things that couples going steady do—most of them, anyway. When they got really to know each other and Shane was no longer so shy and reserved, they had made love.

Not all the way—he wouldn't have done that to a girl like Shane—but near enough for him to believe she loved him and wanted him, too. There'd been a warmth, an eagerness in her that could set him crazy just thinking about her.

Then the whole damned world had come crashing in around him, with his mother's suicide. So great then had been his hatred for the bastard who was his father through accident of birth that he had actually feared he might kill him. He had to get away from Tarant for a while, leaving Shane behind, breaking his own heart and maybe hers, too, but scared of the way everything had gotten all screwed around inside him. Likely Shane would have been better off if he'd stayed away and let her alone, but he couldn't get her out of his mind. He went back for her, and maybe that was the first of a lot of bad mistakes.

Looking back, he had to admit he'd been pretty dumb about women, in many ways. He had tried desperately to make it up to his mother for the way her life had been, even if sometimes he was disgusted with the abject way she yearned over the Bible-spouting, womanizing evangelist she was married to. Court had even entered theological seminary to please her, trying his best but knowing deep inside him that it wasn't right for him, even if in those days he did believe some things that he didn't believe anymore.

Ma had always tried in her plaintive way to discourage him from having anything to do with women. When he started seeing so much of Shane she had warned, "Son, be very sure it isn't just lust you feel for that girl." It had enraged him and he felt like yelling at her, "Hell, yes, I feel lust for her; it's one of the reasons I want to marry her!" but he hadn't answered her at all. He knew she was only trying to safeguard him against the sinful appetites which beset his father. Christ, nobody had to tell him that. He had plenty of the old man in him and he knew it, but there was no way Shane was ever going to be made to suffer for it.

He'd gone on doing the best he could, more certain all the time that no part of the ministry was for him, hoping there'd be some way to get himself off the hook without hurting his mother anymore than she had already been hurt. He knew what she wanted, for him to atone for what she called his father's sins against God by being God's man in a way his father never was. The plain truth was he'd let her brainwash him. *"Make mamma proud of you, son!"* Maybe in a way she hadn't intended she'd made a hypocrite of him, too, because if he had ever faced up to it squarely, inside himself he'd never intended to spend his life behind a pulpit.

In the end none of it had mattered, because

everything he'd tried to do to make up to ma for her unhappiness had been a failure. She'd let him know that loud and clear—lying dead with a bullet through her head—leaving him no way to cleanse himself of all the hatred and rage, but to write God off once and for all and strike out on his own. He'd tried to wipe ma out of his mind as cleanly as if she had never existed. Sometimes he thought, without understanding it fully, that she was easier to forget than his old man had been, because of the hatred for him that was like some kind of rotten sickness.

None of the hell he had muddled through and at last put behind him had been as bad as the ultimate pain of realizing his marriage was a failure, too, and not knowing what to do about it. Too often in his frustration he grew angry and quarreled with Shane, when what he really wanted to do was hold her close and weep the bitter tears he had been unable to shed since he was a kid.

He didn't know anymore, how Shane felt about him. Maybe she felt nothing at all; that was the way it had seemed a lot of the time in these past few years. Sometimes he wondered if she ever remembered how much fun they'd had in the beginning, the way they'd been happy just to be together, and how they'd laughed a lot. Maybe that was what was lacking—the fun. He'd given most of himself and his time to building up his business—making money; fulfilling a vow to himself that Shane was going to have the best of everything.

He recalled, guiltily, that there were things Shane liked for which he hadn't had the time or the inclination. Music. Shane wasn't much for religion, but she loved the choirs in the big churches downtown. *Christ, I'd even go to church with her now, if it would make her happier.* Dancing—he'd always known she loved that, and the only reason he had resisted was that he had two left feet and was no good at it. He felt like a damned fool on a dance floor, but if it would have pleased her, it wouldn't have hurt him to try.

Those were surface things, the tip of the iceberg, and he knew it. He was trying to face up to the fact that although he had said everything he did was for Shane, he'd been blind to a lot of things. Money didn't mean as much to her as to him. Maybe he'd never tried hard enough to understand the things which meant most to her. She had wanted babies, and she had tried desperately to have them. It was too late for that now, but there must be ways of making up to her for the loss.

What was important was that she was coming back to him. Maybe things would be better now.

One thing was certain, he was going to do his damnedest to try to make them better.

He left the downtown traffic and got into the early rush on the freeway. Twenty minutes of that and he was on the Regency off ramp, heading for home. It was only when he turned in at his own house, wheels churning the wet gravel of the driveway, that he realized he had forgotten to stop somewhere and eat. Well, the dining room at the club would be open, maybe he'd drop over there for a steak. He had been staying away while Shane was gone, because it bothered him for people to ask about her. Now he could say, "She's coming home tomorrow."

The thought was comforting to his tired mind.

4.
(Shane)

When dinner was ready she wandered restlessly on to the terrace to wait for the men. It would be nice if she and Jeff could have this evening alone to say their good-byes, but Father Francis had more or less invited himself, and apparently they must make the most of his determined chaperonage.

Jeff said, between annoyance and amusement, "Poor Uncle Francis. He keeps trying to lock the barn door and hoping the horse hasn't already been stolen."

It was strange, now that her brief idyll with Jeff Kendall was ending, the way things were turning themselves around. That their affair was without a future had been implicit between them from the beginning. When it was over there were to be no regrets, no guilt—and no penalty. Of course Father Francis, an unyielding believer in the consequences humans must pay for their transgressions, would shake his head sadly at such optimism.

She was tense and uptight at the thought of saying good-bye to Jeff and wanted only to be able to do it gracefully. It needed finality, like a clean sharp *period*, not the incomplete ending of a comma which left one feeling there should be more.

It was the priest who was bringing the unwanted tension into the situation. It was almost as if she had taken a word from his mind: adultery. But that was only a word, syllables strung together to make an ugly sound. It must be that some sins, like some beauty, were only in the eye of the beholder.

If I had it all to do over I would do it in precisely the same way, so there you are, dear Father Francis, and you may consign me to your precious purgatory if you like, or worse. It has been worth it!

She sat in the swing and let the breeze, still bearing the fragrance of sun-baked pine, fan against her. The weather was mild for October in the mountains, the little night wind redolent of the pleasantly rich tang of decaying leaves. The nocturnal musicians were tuning up, frogs in the shallows sounding their bass notes, crickets fiddling shrill arpeggios. Somewhere along the dark water a loon cried once and was silenced by the mournful echo wavering back from the darkening hills. A vagrant breeze riffled the surface of the lake and on the horizon one star came out and shone brightly. Dimly visible in the misty twilight was the small pine-clad island near which she had fished with Jeff.

At noon we went onto the island and spread our picnic lunch on the beach. Then we walked through the trees and in a clearing where the sun was bright and warm and the earth smelled like cinnamon sticks, we made love.

Tomorrow all this would end. She would be back in the house on Regency Road, cleaning and marketing and preparing meals. There would be the routine days, the piffling interruptions. Milly

Eastman would telephone or drop by—this year she was chairman of the Regency Artists' Association, a thankless task which Shane had gratefully relinquished last year.

Milly would be full of peevish complaints. "It's almost time for the annual art festival and that Trowbridge woman—you know her, Shane, she does those god-awful marine things—insists it's her turn to have the one-man show at the center and my God, if I let her, I'll be laughed right out of Regency!"

Shane would try to soothe her, with patience and tact, resisting the urge to point out that it made little enough difference who was hung, since they were all amateurs and all god-awful, if it came to that. They were products of "art classes" conducted by a woman painter who, Shane suspected, had never been quite good enough to cut it professionally, but she made starkly professional sounds and collected handsome fees, and her students were devout disciples.

Well, them as can does and them as can't teaches!

Shane's own paintings were hung at the center. She had no illusion regarding her work. Most of it was watercolor, airy and delicate and nice to look at for the viewer who did not have too discerning an eye. True, it was better than most of the picture-postcard stuff turned out by

Regency artists, and therefore subject to the most profoundly analytic criticism by her peers; but hers was only a pretty little talent which had already peaked out, and she knew it.

Court was laconic when people spoke admiringly to him about his wife's work. "Well, it makes a nice little hobby for her."

True, and it was a useful hobby, of course, in that it permitted her to contribute something to the Regency way of life, and that was important to Court, who was running to catch up with something.

This was the way of life from which she had fled two months ago and to which she would return tomorrow, a changed Shane in a tight little plastic world which would have changed not one whit. How would that work out? She made a pushing-away gesture as if to keep the old things from closing in on her. The art classes and the exercise classes and the yoga classes, housework and marketing, the committees, the Millys; Dee Andreas, who lived next door, dashing in with her assorted bits of Regency gossip which never seemed really malicious because they were always funny; evenings at home with Court, when they would sit and read or watch Court's favorite television programs... It was not that he was selfish about it, only that Shane loathed virtually everything on the tube and had small preference to express.

Would it be then as if none of this had ever really happened and she had only dreamed someone like Jeff Kendall, the sound of his voice, the feel of his body against hers? Awakening to his nearness, turning her head on the pillow and looking into his face ... making love to him in the flood of morning sunlight across the bed ...

Court and I never made love in the daylight. Court was never very versatile. Sex is necessary to him but it's more like a necessary evil, and I think he is embarrassed by it.

And Shane?

Well, Shane had always been able to take it or leave it, until she met Jeff Kendall.

The Shanes of this world, she thought, rarely got together with the Jeff Kendalls. Maybe that was their trouble.

She did not permit herself to dwell on the right or wrong of her affair with Jeff, neither did she feel she had been influenced by the fact that these days, extramarital sex was regarded by some as the order of things rather than the exception. There were Regency wives who slept around. Everyone knew it. Some of them clearly wanted it known, or at least didn't care who knew. There was gossip about mate-swapping, and there was said to be a very private and select key club whose men members tossed their house keys into the punch bowl at the end of a night's partying. Each woman drew a key from the bowl and went home with the male whose key she had drawn. One could count the evening a loss, Shane supposed wryly, if the key she drew turned out to fit her own front door.

She had listened to these stories with a kind of impersonal contempt, neither quite believing nor disbelieving. The thought of sleeping with a man for whom she felt no emotional attachment, as casually as a bitch in heat, repelled her. It frightened her, too, because it brutalized sex, was almost vicious in its cynical flouting of common decency.

In no way, she affirmed staunchly, did her affair with Jeff Kendall identify her with those other Regency wives.

From somewhere on the road which climbed the hill back of the cottage a car was coming down. Its lights flashed briefly from a curve, throwing into bold relief the slender white trunks of the aspens edging the lane. Then the light was gone and the trees stood dark again, but an unbidden, unwelcome memory had thrust itself into Shane's mind. She closed her eyes, as if the night shadows alone could not cover what she had seen.

"I'm sorry to have to tell you this, boy, but your mother is dead," said the sheriff's officer, a stocky aging man in a brown uniform, pity in his eyes that were long accustomed to looking on grievous things. Court struck his clenched fists repeatedly and savagely against an aspen trunk, his face white and agonized. "I guess it's best I tell you the rest of it now, before you go home. You'll have to know soon enough anyhow. She—shot herself."

It had been Shane who led Court into this cottage, who bathed and bound his torn bloody hands. She was seventeen, and death and violence were strange to her. She was caught up helplessly in the horror of what was happening to Court, and she kept whispering to him, "I'm so sorry, so sorry—"

"God damn him, it was him!" The boy's voice was raw and ugly and the girl knew he was speaking of his father. "Him and his goddamned women!"

At the funeral six of Court's fellow seminary students were pallbearers, and more students crowded into the little chapel, because Court was well liked and his friends were shocked and concerned for him.

Court spoke to no one. He sat unmoving, staring dry eyed at the gray casket with the floral offerings heaped about it. The service was brief, the minister clearly ill at ease. How do you commend to the rewards of eternal life the soul departed of its own volition, summarily rejecting the gift of life on earth? He fumbled self-consciously with words which said nothing reassuring, prayed God's mercy and forgiveness for the departed and comfort for the bereaved, and sounded his final amen with an almost audible relief.

At the cemetery there was the terrifying ultimateness of the newly heaped mound, the rawness of its earth not quite hidden by the flowers. Down there was Court's mother, alone now, her unhappiness at rest with her.

Court made a blind gesture with his arms as if to gather it all to him, the blooms and the raw earth and the defeated woman who had been his mother. Then he lifted his eyes and saw his father, standing apart with bowed head. "You rotten son of a bitch!" The boy's voice slammed into the stillness. "You ever come near me as long as you live, I swear to God I'll kill you."

Shane drew her breath in sharply. Forget it! That was nearly eleven years ago. It has nothing to do with now.

When she had come to Shadow Lake two months ago she had been very certain she was going to ask Court for a divorce. That he would be angry, his pride hurt, she knew, but she wondered wearily if he, too, might not be relieved to have the whole sorry business over with.

Now she was going back to him and she could not be certain when she had reached that decision or what had brought her to it. She did not want to be a divorcée. That carried a connotation of failure and a possible projection of the future.

If there were a future for her with Jeff Kendall, then what might have been her decision? Not to leave Court at all. To simply give up on a failing marriage is one thing. To leave him for another man, to end ten years of marriage with the same betrayal that had sent his mother to her death—I could never do that to Court.

Wouldn't Court say that you have already betrayed him?

He'll never know. Now at least I have some insight into my own needs and I can try to understand his.

She rejected that at once, appalled at what it implied. Taking what she had learned from Jeff and offering it to Court, as if Jeff were some sort of surrogate—*My God, what kind of woman are you?*

That Court loved her in his own way she was certain. She was equally certain he was not sufficiently sensitive to her to discern any change which he could not attribute to the improvement in her general health due to her lengthy rest. He would accept her return matter-of-factly, having never doubted that she would return, having never guessed that she had for one moment considered not returning.

Along the lake someone or something had startled the night creatures and they fell silent. Presently Shane heard voices. The men were coming in together. She could hear the priest speaking, and Jeff's deeper tones in reply.

When they came onto the terrace, Shane studied the priest, and declined to feel ashamed of her little sense of antagonism.

I don't like the clergy. The bad ones, like Court's father, are disgusting. The good ones, like Father Francis, make me feel all my sins are showing, like little flags flying.

She didn't know much about Catholics, of course, but she had heard about the confession bit.

Father, I have sinned. I've been sleeping with a relative of yours—

An involuntary giggle escaped her. The two men looked questioningly at her and she stifled the giggle to say politely, "Sorry, it was a private joke."

The priest said, "Sorry we're late, Shane. It's

such a fine evening, we walked over, and we've been battling every step of the way."

"You and Jeff battling? I can't imagine it." She put the proper note of cheerful banter into it. "You're just in time. Would you like to eat out here on the terrace?"

"Sounds great. Why not put us to work? We'll help bring things out."

"Fair enough. If you want aprons you'll find them hanging beside the kitchen cupboard."

"Me, in an apron?" Jeff lifted an eyebrow. "What if some of my more manly students were to see me?"

Father Francis laughed and said, "Now you're being a chauvinist. Come along and get your apron."

He went into the cottage, but Jeff hung back to say in a low voice, "Keep your guard up, he's been asking questions. Not directly, only leading enough to give me the opportunity to unburden my soul if I felt the need."

"Jeff, I don't like that."

"Well, it's your good he's most concerned with. If the piece must have a villain, I expect I'm it." He followed his uncle, whistling a little tune. Shane thought irritably, As long as Father Francis chooses to be a practically uninvited guest at our last dinner together, he might have the grace to mind his own business. One would think he'd know that if his efforts to keep us out of bed together have been futile up to now, it's much too late to improve on them.

She wondered if he suspected that on more than one night when Jeff drove away from his uncle's cottage, ostensibly to return to Tarant, he had simply parked his car in an abandoned shed on the back of Shane's property and returned to her afoot.

Throughout the meal she was silent for the most part, listening to the two men arguing amiably. They bore a resemblance physically, and in the stubbornness of their individual convictions. Actually, Jeff was only a lapsed Catholic, but the relationship had brought him up against considerable opposition at the strictly Protestant college in Tarant.

Shane was a Tarant girl herself. Her uncle had been dean of the theological school in the small college which had been even then struggling for survival in a rapidly changing academic world. Founded by Uncle Gregory's grandfather, it was endowed by its own stolidly fundamentalist church, a relatively small splinter group which affiliated itself with none of the older, more established churches. Tarant College placed emphasis on its seminary and for years its liberal-arts department attracted chiefly young men who planned to study for the fundamentalist ministry or, Shane appended wryly, girls who planned to study to be fundamentalist ministers' wives.

On the wider educational scene in those days the school might as well have been nonexistent. The seminary's academic entrance requirements were too negligible, the broader curriculum too neglected. Uncle Gregory had stoutly maintained that for one to preach the Word of God, one needed only a thorough knowledge of that Word, and to attain to such knowledge only one text was of any ultimate value.

Uncle Gregory and most of his fellows were dead and gone now and change was coming to Tarant College; that was clear—witness one professor, Doctor Jeffrey Kendall, an irreverent agnostic with Catholic connections.

"I had the devil's own time," he had related to Shane with relish, "persuading the regents I wasn't a Papist spy come to raise hell with their pure Protestant establishment."

"You must have used some gold-plated persuasion. There was a time not too long ago when you couldn't have got a foot in the door, not with your pagan beginnings."

"Well, fortunately for me they were trying to increase their enrollment and get state funding. To do that they had to upgrade the curriculum, and they were up against it for qualified personnel, what with most of the good men opting for better-paying schools. Tarant suited me because it offers me the chance to get in some research and writing. As a matter of fact, I like it and I plan to stay for a while, if I don't fall afoul of some of the hardnoses who'd like to see my heathen hide nailed to the barn door."

Shane could fancy Uncle Gregory stirring uneasily in his crypt at the idea of a modernist (she could almost hear him spew the word) holding a chair here. As long as Uncle Gregory had lived he had grimly resisted certain change and rather than see Tarant "liberalized"—the word to him was one with blasphemy and perdition—he would see it in a fundamentalist grave.

Ironically enough, Jeff had scant religious leaning in any direction and this, together with his all-but-gone Catholicism, was a thorn in the flesh to his own uncle, a point for frequent debate between them. Recently Jeff had published a paper which had received considerable praise from fellow scholars, and Father Francis was determined to attribute to it a spiritual flavor which Jeff impatiently denied. They argued it heatedly; they were, in fact, going at it this very moment, their animated voices swirling about Shane.

The priest was insisting, "Disregarding any conscious intent on your part, your work does betray an innate reliance on certain religious values. Call them spiritual, if you prefer."

"Nonsense. My job," Jeff pointed a celery stick at his uncle, "is to equate human emotion with human motivation and behavior. If in the process I turn up something a fellow human finds encouraging or elevating, well and good, but I don't write with a view to that end." He grinned at his uncle. "You're beautiful, you know that? A dedicated, one-track mind—I honestly think you'd love it if being religious were against the law, and then all the faithful would have to stand up and be counted."

His uncle said dryly, "You'd be safe enough at any rate. They'd have to prove it on you, and I don't think they could make a case against you. I do suspect you may be required to do your stint in purgatory turning out endless essays on the sin of denying the good that is in you." He turned an innocent smile on Shane. "Don't you agree, my dear?"

"I'm afraid you two lost me quite awhile ago. I've only the vaguest notion what you're talking about."

"Anyway, Uncle Francis, Shane isn't of your faith. What would she know about purgatory?"

"The truth is," she rejoined, tartly, "Shane is of no particular faith at all. If you'll excuse me, I'll bring the dessert." She escaped into the kitchen, feeling annoyed with herself and with the priest. She had felt an urge to be rude, if only obliquely, and wasn't he being oblique in his turn, expounding on the "good" in one? Or was that only her conscience sitting in as interpreter?

If I were to get myself and my life together, Jeff would be the best thing that ever happened to me. I have loved being with him. Good and bad have nothing to do with it, and I will not be moralized to.

It was silly, of course, being annoyed. The priest was a good man, and if he was aware of her affair with his nephew and considered it a sin, well then, wasn't that his job, disapproving of sin?

When she returned to the table the conversation had drifted to other topics. They sat over their after-dessert coffee, talking desultorily, falling into silences, watching the stars deepen in intensity above the hills. The priest was the first to stir himself.

"A fine dinner, Shane. I'll miss your cooking almost as much as your company. Jeffrey tells me you're taking the early flight from Tarant in the morning. I'm driving down myself; my bishop is in town and I've orders to present myself. May I offer you my service as chauffeur?"

Jeff intervened promptly, "No way. I'm coming up to drive her down myself."

If his uncle saw anything incongruous in the proposition in Jeff's driving the thirty winding miles up the mountain in early morning only to drive down again when there was transportation readily available for Shane, he did not comment. He said only, "Well, then, it's getting late and I'm sure she has last-minute things to do, so we'd better get along and let her be at them."

"You go along and get your beauty rest," Jeff's voice was bland, "so you'll be all bright eyed and bushy tailed for the bishop. I'll stick around and help Shane clear up."

When the priest had said good-bye and gone away, Shane stood beside the open door, the lamplight from within falling across her frown. "That was pretty obvious, wasn't it? He can hardly help guessing you'll spend the night here."

"How else was I to get rid of him?" He was standing at the top of the terrace steps, watching the glow of the priest's flashlight bob along the pathway through the trees.

Shane said presently, "You'd better go over to his place after a little while and pick up your car. If it's still parked in his driveway in the morning he'll hardly need it spelled out for him, will he? You know, it is pretty silly, two grown people playing a kind of hide-and-seek with him, and for what? What could he have done, even if he had known for sure?"

92

"Nothing, of course. If I were one of his parishioners, he'd probably be on my tail. As it is, I'm only an unregenerate relative, so all he can do is fret. He's relieved you're going home tomorrow, and he doesn't want anything to happen between us tonight that might change your plans. Anyway, he's a sweet guy and there's no point in hurting him if it can be avoided."

"Well, we've certainly gone to considerable lengths to avoid it." Conscious of the sharp edge to her voice, she added, "You're right, of course, it's just that he keeps touching a nerve on the subject of good and bad. Would it ease his mind any, d'you think, if he knew you haven't even asked me to stay?"

"Shane, do you think that's quite fair?"

She shook her head. "No, it isn't. Let's just pretend I didn't say it."

When the night grew chilly they built a fire on the hearth and sat before it. Resting in the stillness with her head against Jeff's shoulder, Shane stared into the flames. She heard the ticking of the old Seth Thomas on the mantel and felt a need to hold back the moving hands. Not to keep her here with Jeff, only to hold back tomorrow for a little while.

I can settle for what we've had together and let him go out of my life. I think I've already done that in my own mind. But if I were going on from here alone I think it might be easier. It's the going back that I dread.

She stirred and said, "I telephoned Court this afternoon to tell him I'm coming home. I keep trying to think what it will be like. Everything will be changed, but only for me—or will they see a difference in me, do you think?"

"How can I tell you that when I don't know what you're like at home?"

"I doubt you'd like me much. I'm there. I function. I go through the motions."

"Do you enjoy putting yourself down?"

"Is that what I'm doing?" She twisted about in his arms to look at him. "You know, I remember your asking me a strange thing when we first got to know each other. 'Why do you dislike yourself?' you said. It annoyed me because I thought you were playing the psychologist."

"Sorry about that."

"Well, what you said was true, I guess. There was a time not so long ago when I was very sick of *me*. My doctor even gave it a name. Poor David, I'm certain he thought I needed psychiatric help, and maybe I did. He was the one who persuaded me to come here. I think he hoped the solitude might give me a chance to take a good look and recognize it for myself—that I needed help, I mean."

"Did it frighten you?"

"The idea of psychiatric treatment? Yes, I'm sure it did. After all, what truths about me might it uncover that I don't want to know?" She gave a little laugh. "Sometimes I'd try to imagine what things a psychiatrist might ask me, and how I'd answer him."

"And how did you come off best, as doctor or patient?"

Calmly, she rejoined, "You're poking fun at me."

"No such thing. I really want to know."

"I'm afraid I wasn't much good as the patient. I was too much on the defensive. They do go back, don't they? Like 'What do you remember about your parents? Were they kind to you? How did you feel about them?'"

Jeff said, "Why don't you tell me?" and at her questioning look, "I'm serious. You and I have talked about a lot of things, but you've never really told me much about yourself. When you're gone, I'll wonder."

After a moment she nodded. "All right, I'll play the game with you. Let me see, what do I remember about my parents—?"

5.

"Shane, what in the name of heaven is wrong with you?" Her mother's voice was cool, laced with disapproval. "I don't know what to do with you, creating this absurd scene when you know perfectly well your father and I have these commitments in New York."

"Why can't I come with you this time?" asked small Shane, standing before her parent to plead stubbornly, and futilely.

"Your father would never permit you to stay out of school, you know that. It isn't as if you hadn't stayed with Grandmother Parker before. Really, you are old enough to begin to learn a little self-reliance." Her mother drew on gloves, adjusted her furs, and the child knew the interview was ending. "Now, dry your eyes and we'll have no more of this nonsense."

"You don't love me." Wild sobbing. "You don't love me at all, and neither does papa!"

Margot Parker said, calmly, "Your father and I love you, but you do make it difficult for me to like you when you behave like this."

They went away. There was a story about them in the newspaper, and their picture: a brilliant, well-known team, John and Margot Parker, globe-trotting missionaries, correspondents, photographers, the only celebrities to whom Tarant could lay claim. They had been awarded some international recognition or other and were off to New York to be honored by fellow journalists.

At school the teacher showed the news story and picture to the class, and spoke admiringly of Shane's parents.

"You're a very lucky little girl," she said.

"How proud you must be of them."

"I'm not," said Shane, in a loud clear voice. "I hate them."

"It was rotten of me, I know." She withdrew from Jeff's arms and sat a little apart from him as if to isolate herself with a shameful memory. "But I was always so lonely. My grandmother was old and children made her nervous. I was supposed to be very quiet and was never allowed to invite the neighbor children in. I couldn't accept their invitations, either, because that meant one must ask them in return. Still, to have said that I hated my parents—" She shook her head. "I'm sure the other kids went home and told their folks; anyway it got back to Grandmother Parker that I had said it and she made me feel awful about it. It was—I don't know—as if I'd wished them dead. You see, they never came home again. Their plane crashed."

Because Grandmother Parker was too aged and frail to have permanent responsibility for a small girl, Shane went into the home of Uncle Gregory, papa's considerably older brother.

Uncle Gregory had admired papa and mama, although he deplored a certain worldliness in them. Of course, to Uncle Gregory only scholarliness and high morality were important. He could abide stupidity and sin in no one, although Shane sometimes had the confused impression that to him a stupid sin must carry a more severe penalty than one commited by an intellectual.

Uncle Gregory was a formidable figure, respected and feared on the campus and at home. To the child he was a shadowy, almost menacing figure, to be avoided whenever possible, obeyed at all costs. She learned to be very quiet and self-effacing when he was on the premises.

Those were drab years for her, so unendingly alike that in retrospect she could call to mind little to distinguish one from another. Her only times of contentment were those she spent here at Shadow Lake, in this cottage which had belonged to the family. Here she was free to wander as she chose and she knew the countryside by heart, the lake's moods, the sunlight dancing like diamonds on its rippled surface, its sudden black storms.

That the lake was sanctuary for her was due partly to the fact that Uncle Gregory rarely came here. She and Aunt Grace came alone. The latter was a pallid, retiring sort of woman. Her world was bounded on all sides by her husband and she would not have dreamed of opposing him in anything. She and Shane were never really close. Perhaps to her the child was a duty seen, a duty done, although she was always kind in her quiet way.

Shane had learned, early on, to be her own companion. She was musically inclined and, in encouragement of the inclination, her parents had purchased a violin for her when she was almost too tiny to be able to clutch the instrument. Through her adolescent years she studied with whatever teachers were available at the college. She always took her violin to the lake with her, wandering abroad with it, sometimes playing what she heard, the call of a bird, the whistle of the wind through pines; or what she saw, a towering thundercloud, the positions of blackbirds resting on the musical staff formed by five telephone wires which ran along the lake road.

She was what Uncle Gregory called fanciful, and she knew it was not a particularly complimentary characterization. In her violin case she carried a roll of sketching paper and a notebook for drawing, or jotting down impressions as they came to her.

In later years she would come upon an excerpt from an "imagining" she had written one wild evening when a threatening storm rolled up from the west. Its clouds had jagged torn places in them from which dying sunlight dropped scattered patches of gold onto the earth. Then one by one these patches disappeared, and it seemed to Shane as if someone unseen were walking about to pick them up. She had written:

The day is a handsome child. Sometimes he is in good humor and gets out of bed all golden and smiling. Sometimes he is sulky and cries and that is what makes the rain. The night is his black nursemaid. When she has put him into bed she goes about softly, picking up the bright playthings he has dropped and laying them away until morning. . . .

In that afteryear Shane would be half self-embarrassed, half pitying of the lonely child who had written those words, and with a little laugh would drop the scrap of paper into the fire.

For her, Shadow Lake was touched with magic the year around, from the delicate greens of spring to the rioting colors of autumn. Most of all she loved walking in autumn rain, when flaming scarlet and gold leaves shamed the gray of the sulking skies and the dark wet tree trunks intensified the vividness of their foliage.

As much as she loved the lake she hated the town, especially in winter when the skies were leaden and the snow in the streets was churned to ugly slush by passing wheels. Then the rooms of Uncle Gregory's austere house smelled of wet galoshes and wool and burning gas logs, and winter was a heartless jailer imprisoning Shane within the narrow and uninspired corridor which led endlessly from home to school and back again.

And to chapel.

Most of all she had hated going to chapel, for it was there she spent long hours listening to Uncle Gregory's stern voice mapping out the joyless life one must lead in order to attain heaven; or suffering with young neophyte ministers stumbling through painstakingly prepared and badly delivered sermons designed more to please Uncle Gregory than to invoke divine approval. All of them presented heaven as the uninviting alternative to a burning hell, in which she was never quite able to believe, even though her skepticism did give her vague feelings of guilt and apprehension.

One needed to believe in something, of course. It seemed to her that if she had an Our-Father-which-art-in-heaven who really and truly cared what happened to her, at least she had more going for her up there than she had down here. In any case, she simply could not believe the things Uncle Gregory believed, although she was repeatedly exhorted to believe, if she would be saved—

"Saved for what?" She asked it more of herself than of Jeff. "All those ghastly gates of gold and streets paved with the stuff, and people running around like idiots, twanging on harps—I used to think it sounded gruesome, and I'd be lucky not to have to go there. But would you believe that even after all these years, talking this way makes me feel a little nervous? Uncle Gregory would say I'm blaspheming. Are you getting tired of hearing about Uncle Gregory?"

"No, but I can understand how you must have gotten pretty tired of him."

"Well, what was so scary was that I knew he honestly believed every bit of it, about heaven and hell and how this world is meant to be a vale of tears and suffering and people aren't supposed to be happy in this life. I knew Uncle Gregory was a very wise man and if he believed it and I didn't, then there must be something wrong with me. His church preached a kind of predestination and I guess I felt I was one of those born to be damned, so there wasn't any point in trying."

"So you never got saved."

"Not so you'd notice it." Her little laugh was suddenly self-conscious. "One of my biggest hang-ups was the happiness bit. It seemed to me happy people weren't nearly so apt to do bad things to each other, like making war or robbing and murdering, so if God would just let them be happy and not punish them for it, they'd want to be good. Even if I could have believed in the kind of God Uncle Gregory did, I'd have hated Him. Do you know, when I was little, whenever I was in bed, no matter how uncomfortably warm it was, I had to be covered—because I didn't want God to look at me when I was asleep. I suppose it sounds crazy, but some of the things that made me afraid and depressed then, still do, to this day."

"It isn't crazy. Man concocts a 'truth' and force-feeds it to hungry souls, who end up with an indigestible glob of guilt and uncertainty. A man who does that to a child deserves to go to whatever kind of hell it is he believes in. I don't think God intended it to be that way."

She asked, surprised, "Do *you* believe in God?" and he gave a little shout of laughter.

"Did you think I don't?"

"You don't talk as if you do."

"Actually, I don't talk about it at all. It's a private thing. You know, I read once that God must be less offended by an out-and-out atheist than he is by some of man's organized religions. Anyway, how do you choose between a thousand and one faiths and be sure you've made a proper choice? Personally, I don't believe God plays a game of guess-which-hand-I've-hidden-it-in." He gave her a wry grin. "There you have it in a very small capsule, the Kendall theory—and welcome to it."

"Well, I believe in God, too. Anyway, I think I do. Only sometimes I wish it didn't just sort of trail off there; for me, anyway. There needs to be something more." Suddenly she gave a little laugh. "Does it strike you as funny, our sitting here talking so solemnly about things like God and religion, and sin—?"

"Because any minute now we're going to tumble into bed together? Look, sex and religion are two of man's biggest hang-ups. I've an idea both are here to stay and for the protagonists of either to try to sweep the other under the rug is pretty damned stupid." Then he switched topics abruptly:

"Tell me about Court." And when she did not reply at once he leaned forward to look intently at her. "You never talk about him. Does it make you feel disloyal?"

"No. I don't know. What has he to do with us?"

"He's a part of what makes Shane run, and that's what we're talking about."

She reflected, briefly. "I don't mind talking about him, but he is his own person, and I wouldn't want anything I said to give you a wrong impression of him."

"The only impression I have is that you're not happy with him, but that doesn't necessarily tell me anything about him, does it?"

"Maybe I'd better explain a little more about me. The answers to some of the questions might be there, and then you wouldn't have to ask them."

"You don't like to have me ask you questions?"

"Not ones I can't answer. It makes me feel you might think I know the answer and just don't want to face it."

That was what Doctor David Price had said, *"About all a psychiatrist could do for you would be to help you figure out what the problem is, and I've an idea you already know."*

She said, candidly, "I like the way our relationship has been. I'd hate for there to be anything clinical about it."

"I like our relationship, too, and as for its being clinical—no way. But you're ending it tomorrow, going back to where you came from. Maybe I'd like to feel that because of our relationship you've got a clearer shot at happiness."

"It's just that I want to be fair to Court. I—do love him, always have." She hesitated, then said, "Court was the first real boyfriend I ever had. Uncle Gregory was always so critical, and I guess I preferred loneliness to having him pick my friends to pieces. Actually, I didn't mind being alone. I had my own interests—the lake, sketching, my music."

"You mentioned that you played violin. Do you still?"

"I have one, but I rarely touch it. Court

doesn't care for fiddle music; that's what he calls it. And that," there was a defensive shading to her tone, "doesn't necessarily tell you anything about him, either. A lot of people don't care for strings."

"I belong to that group myself. Unless you're pretty good, it squeaks."

"I was pretty good, and I never squeaked. Well, hardly ever. Anyway, I loved to draw and paint, and fool around with writing. I made up a true story once."

"Isn't that a little ambiguous?"

"You know, one of those first-person things that are supposed to have really happened. A girl I knew used to buy those magazines, and I read some of them. I sent my story to one of them and do you know what? They paid me fifty dollars for it!" She bent forward in sudden mirth. "Uncle Gregory found out about it somehow. He made me let him read it, and you should have heard him! It *was* pretty awful. I said I was this high-school girl who'd gotten pregnant by the campus football hero—" She could not go on and they collapsed against each other, rocking with laughter.

"How old were you?"

"Sixteen. It was in my senior year in high school. Uncle Gregory wouldn't believe I'd simply got my ideas from those other stories. He said you don't get that kind of carnal knowledge—that's what he called it—just from reading about it. I guess I did apply quite a lot of imagination to what it might be like, being seduced by an attractive boy."

"I've a girl in one of my classes who could tell you about that—only in her case I expect it was she who did the seducing. Never mind, go on."

"Well, anyway, it was fun, even if it did get me prayed over."

"No matter if it was a bad story, someone did buy it. Did you ever try writing anything else for publication?"

"No. I always thought to write professionally would take more than simply a way with words—ambition, too. I never had that to any degree, or ego, whatever you want to call it. I felt too overshadowed by all the eggheads around me to dare poke my own head up. There was a thing I'd have liked to try—I'd planned to do it for my own children if I had any—a child's book, with my own illustrations."

"Couldn't you still do it? I'd think if it were fresh and innovative there'd be a demand for it."

"It's a highly specialized field, and I suppose I simply lacked the drive to try for it." Court wouldn't want me to. He has always resented anything alien to his own interests. I suspect he feels threatened somehow. "I think no sort of professional life ever really appealed to me. I wanted a family, and it seemed to me career people don't have time for their own children. I know mine hadn't.

"Anyway, I wasn't quite seventeen when I entered Tarant College. I had hoped desperately that Uncle Gregory would send me away somewhere—at least to a girls' school—but he wouldn't hear of me going anywhere but Tarant, and living at home. College was pretty much like high school had been. I made high marks in all my courses, which must have pleased my uncle, although he would never have said so."

It was odd, the way there had been the nagging little need to please Uncle Gregory, if only in some small way, perhaps to prove that she was not completely beyond redemption. Once she had won an almost-compliment from him when near the end of her freshman year she had won a top award in a state watercolor competition. It was not, Uncle Gregory conceded, a bad painting, although he could have wished she had chosen a religious subject, more befitting a Tarant student, and a Parker.

"You met Court in college?"

"The very first day of my freshman year, in the registrar's office. I don't know just how to describe him to you. He was very good-looking. He still is. He was full of life, always clowning around, making people laugh. He was a year ahead of me but I'd seen him around, when I'd been on campus for violin or piano lessons. You could tell the girls were silly about him, they were always hanging around him. I'd never even said hello to him. To tell you the truth it surprised me that he paid me any attention at all."

"Why?"

"Because I was such a mouse. Boys just didn't notice me, or at least the only ones who did were mousy themselves. Anyway, that very first day Court bought me a hamburger at the student union, and he asked me to go to chapel with him on Sunday. I'd never struck up an acquaintance that fast in my life but he sort of swept me along. I loved it. I admired him because he was so friendly and outgoing; people were always saying what a marvelous minister he was going to make."

"Good God!" He was genuinely horrified. "Don't tell me I've been bedding down with a dominie's lady!"

"Don't be silly, of course not. Court is in business, but he was a seminary student when I met him. I don't think he ever really wanted to be a minister; he was doing it to please someone else." A slight frown creased her forehead. "It isn't easy to explain what he was like in those days. When I got to know him better I realized he wasn't all that outgoing, I mean, he knew how to get along with people and make them like him, but it was as if he didn't really need people, only *someone*. Does that make any sense?"

"I think so."

"His father was a traveling evangelist. In those days he wasn't associated with any church, at least none that I'd heard of. Of course, Waverly now has his own church, down south somewhere, it's one of those radio and television things, and quite widely known—"

"Oh, hell, of course!" Jeff gave an incredulous snort of laughter. "The Manning Voice of Prophecy. No wonder my mind kept playing around with the name. The great Waverly Manning himself. I've heard of him—some of it from the seminary faculty and none of it very complimentary, I'm afraid."

"I'd expect not. Uncle Gregory loathed him. They say Waverly does have a big following now, and that he makes a lot of money. Still, Court always said anyone could take a twenty-five dollar fee and a handful of members and start a tax-exempt church."

"And this guy is your father-in-law."

She shrugged. "We never see or hear from him. Court won't have anything to do with him since his mother died. When I first knew Waverly he had a big tent and went around holding meetings in it, the way they used to do in the old days. I heard him preach once or twice. He wasn't really an educated man but he was bright, handsome. You know, full of magnetic charm—and words."

"And you didn't like him."

"Not much, although I never really saw that much of him. He was away most of the time. Court and his mother were very close and I know it was because of her that he went into the seminary. She was a devout person and I guess it was her dream for her only child to become a real minister. Adele was a nice woman, and I liked her well enough, but there was something pathetic about her. It made me uneasy to be around her. Court was terribly protective of her, and later I could understand why."

Abruptly she withdrew from Jeff and leaned forward, shoulders hunched and her arms hugging her knees.

"It was awful." Her voice was thin with unhappy remembering. "It was in the spring. I remember how much fun life seemed to be just then. Court and I were together all the time, and I suppose I was getting a kick out of knowing I was the envy of a lot of the other girls.

"Anyway, on a Saturday evening we'd come here to the cottage on a picnic with another couple. A sheriff's officer came looking for us, to tell Court his mother was dead. Waverly had told her he was in love with some woman he'd met on one of his revival tours, and they were going away together. Adele walked out of that room where they had been talking, into another room where they kept a loaded gun, and she literally blew her brains out." Shane turned a haunted look to Jeff. "With no thought of what she was doing to Court, not giving him a chance to try to talk to her, or comfort her. It was as if—if she couldn't have that husband of hers, she didn't want Court, either. How could a mother *do* such a thing?"

"People do insane things under stress. The gun was there at hand in her moment of insanity. Given a few moments' time she might have acted differently."

"I always had the feeling it wasn't the first time Waverly had done that sort of thing, and that Court and his mother both knew it."

"Maybe her husband had never threatened leaving her before. Some women can put up with infidelity as long as they don't feel their own position is jeopardized."

"Court and I never discussed it. At first I thought it might help him to talk about it, but he wouldn't. It's as if he has wiped it all completely from his mind."

"He never talks about his mother?"

"Never. Sometimes I've wondered if he felt something of what I did—her letting him down—and couldn't forgive her for it. I don't know."

Shane was silent for a long, remembering moment. Then:

"Court changed, after that. He was miserable and bitter, and at the cemetery he cursed his father. I'm sure that with Adele dead he would have left the seminary anyway, but Uncle Gregory didn't give him a choice. Because of the scene he made at his mother's grave, and the language he used, I think my uncle wanted it on the record that he'd been dismissed. They gave him a summary expulsion without any credits for the years.

"He turned against all churches then. We were married by a justice—Court wouldn't hear of standing up before any minister. To this day he resents it if I attend services. At home, some of the big churches have really magnificent music and I'd enjoy that, but I rarely go. He doesn't actually forbid it, but he lets me know clearly how he feels."

"How did he and your uncle get on before the tragedy? Did Gregory approve of him?"

"Not really. Uncle Gregory had had doubts as to whether Court had actually been called to the ministry, and that was very important—to have the call. He considered Court's attitude irresponsible and lacking in piety. Waverly Manning was so—so flamboyant, I guess that's the word, and probably Uncle Gregory fancied he could see some of that in Court—the attractiveness, the ability to charm people. But by then even Uncle Gregory realized I was getting a bit old to be bossed about, although he let me know he thought Court was wrong for me.

"Looking back, I know nothing could have been the same after the way Adele died. Court was quiet and withdrawn and it was as if I just couldn't get through to him. He didn't even seem to want to kiss me anymore, he seemed ashamed of that part of our relationship. It was funny—in some ways Court treated me the way Uncle Gregory always had, bossing me, deciding where we'd go, what we'd do. If he didn't like someone I liked or something I wore, I'd stop seeing that person or wearing that dress. It was what I was accustomed to, of course, and anyway, it was different with Court than with the others who had dominated me. None of them really wanted me, or at least I thought they didn't. Court did, and it was good, being wanted.

"Court left Tarant suddenly, without even telling me where he was going, I felt terribly alone and rejected, and I was certain he was never coming back. Then I began to be a little ashamed of our relationship—of my part in it, anyway. We'd never actually had sex but we'd come close to it, you know? It was always Court who put on the brakes. I thought he probably despised me for it, knowing I would have let him go as far as he wanted. It was a rotten feeling.

"I adored him, and I was terribly worried about him; and of course I was humiliated, too, certain that everyone knew he had thrown me over. I don't think I've ever been quite so miserable. He did finally come back, of course, and he asked me to marry him. At first I did have some reservations. He was still so changed, so—strange. I suppose if I were to be completely honest, I'd have to say that being with him just wasn't that much fun anymore—but I told myself that it was just that he was still grieving over what had happened and that he just needed time to get back to being his old self again.

"Court had some money from his mother, a trust fund her own father had set up. I think she had refused to give it to Waverly for his church and that caused trouble between them. Anyway, Court had a cousin in California who had a business, and he offered to take Court in with him. Court had decided to invest in the business. He asked me to go with him, and I went."

"Did your uncle ever forgive you?"

"I doubt it. I never saw him again. He died

when Court and I had been married about two years. Aunt Grace outlived him by only a year—poor thing. I've always thought that with Uncle Gregory gone she simply didn't know how to go on living. When he died he left me about thirty thousand dollars. It was a trust fund my parents had set up. He had been entitled to draw on it to help with my education and all that, but he hadn't used a cent and the fund was intact when it passed to me. I suppose it doesn't make any difference now but I wish I had known Uncle Gregory deliberately paid for everything himself in order to leave the inheritance untouched for me. It must have meant he cared a little for me, and I rather needed to know that.

"When Aunt Grace died she left me this lake property. She must have known what it meant to me, and maybe it was her way of showing me an affection she was never able to express. I was sorry for her, but I didn't really grieve for either of them. That made me feel guilty, but then I've felt a great deal of that in my life."

"Guilt for what?"

She made a vague gesture. "I don't know, for being so—maybe just for *being*. Not so long ago I was very ill, and after that things got so they seemed meaningless. There was something so—so essential lacking in me that sometimes I almost doubted I even cast a shadow."

"But you felt Court needed you."

"I suppose I did, but it hasn't been all that great for him, either. I didn't get to be a candidate for psychiatry overnight. He never says much, but I'm sure I drove him up the wall with my moods, sometimes."

"I gather he's been successful in business."

"Oh, yes. He and his cousin were in electronics, sound systems, that sort of thing. Several years ago he combined what he had accumulated with my money, and bought out the business. He has kept expanding Manning Enterprises and it has gotten to be quite a going concern. Court is capable, and ambitious. Money is very important to him. Quite a while ago he was able to withdraw my part of the investment from the firm and put it back into a savings account for me. He has an extremely well-equipped plant, and about thirty employees. It's really quite an impressive operation."

She arose, to move restlessly about the room. "We never had any children, of course. There won't be any. As time went by, we seemed to have less and less in common. I'm sure that was as much my fault as his, maybe more. In some ways he simply outgrew me. We've—had problems. This is the first time I ever cheated on him." She used the phrase calmly. "I'm sure Court never has. He wouldn't think it was honorable. Court is a very decent man." Then she made a sharp gesture of dismissal.

"I'm sorry. I don't want to talk about him anymore."

Jeff got to his feet. "The moon is up. Let's go for a walk along the lake."

Long after Jeff slept quietly beside her Shane was wakeful, considering facts. She reached out a hand to touch the sleeping man but he did not stir. His unconsciousness separated them now the way distance would separate them tomorrow.

Tears stung at her eyelids and she turned her head restlessly on the pillow, staring at the moonlight falling through the window. She tried to summon up the sight and sound of Court, to call back the time when he had been so very dear to her. Those had been bright days, luminous and enchanted. Where had the magic gone?

A fragment of memory flickered across her consciousness like heat lightning on a summer night. Court running along the brow of a hill, tugging at a kite string and laughing at the antics of the captive thing—paper and slender sticks—cavorting high in the air above him... Her spirit had risen, too, filling her with a delightful excitement as if she were up there with the kite, deliciously free, yet not free, bound by invisible threads to the laughing boy.

It was only the promise I felt. We were so terribly young. We made promises to each other that neither of us could keep.

She knew that never again would she be that happy. With Jeff Kendall she had known heady excitement, a physical fulfillment different from anything she had ever felt with Court; but one man could not keep another's promises, and something had already gone out of her, the innocent expectation, the believing.

It was with Court that I wanted to find the fulfillment. That was the promise not kept.

Jeff was full of talk on the way down the mountain. He persisted in dwelling on the matter of Shane's capabilities. "You've let other people diminish your feeling of self-worth long enough. I'd like to believe you're going to involve yourself in something that will have some meaning for you. Do the everyday things you have to do, but leaven the flatness by creating something that's totally yours, uniquely you." He winced at his own rhetoric but went on, "Even if it is only a unique mousetrap."

She demurred. "Even if I had the ability, and you seem more convinced of that than I, I wouldn't know how to begin."

"By beginning. Build something—a painting, a poem, a true story," he gave her a little grin.

"You run it up a flagpole and if nobody salutes it, so what? You may never get rich or famous at it but if you give it everything you've got, it might keep you off a psychiatrist's couch."

"Or out of a psychologist's bed?"

That made him laugh, but he persisted, "If you can't sell your ability, give it away. Get into volunteer work. Take that neglected fiddle of yours and find a place, maybe a children's hospital, where there might be someone who wants to listen, or learn. Do something, for God's sake, even if you do it wrong! You came from brilliant people who starved you emotionally. All right, you wanted to avoid being like them, but there's always a middle ground, you know. In any case, they're all dead and gone and it doesn't matter a damn to them that you've rejected them, so your revenge can't be worth much to you."

"Revenge?" She challenged that, indignantly. "I never wanted revenge on anyone!"

"I think you did. Gregory Parker had a hellish impact on your life, with his deep-freeze intellect. You were a hungry, unhappy kid and you could even the score most completely by totally rejecting your people and their world. You wanted to lose yourself in an utterly different life, even if it turned out to be not much more satisfactory than the world you were running from."

She protested stiffly, "My life with Court hasn't been all *that* bad."

"You're defending what it has been. I'm arguing for what it might be. Reach back to your own people for whatever they gave you that you can use, and stop trying to stuff yourself into a dull mold that doesn't fit you at all. You're rather special to me, Shane. I'd like to think you're going to get it all together."

Presently, moved by some obscure urge to reassure him, she said, "Well, maybe someday there'll be a children's book by Shane Parker Manning and maybe you'll happen to see it, and remember me."

His glance was on the road and he did not look at her. "I'll remember you."

Her flight was being called. Beyond the gate she could see the great silver plane, the smiling stewardess waiting at the top of the ramp to greet them. The morning breeze, sliding out of an October-blue sky, held the first hint of winter riding down from the north. On the flanks of the mountains, aspen and birch and cottonwood laced a fretwork of vivid color against the somber green pines, and sumac lighted its autumn fires on the lower hillsides.

Shane stood memorizing it all with hungry eyes. She thought of the cottage, standing closed and silent now, with only the murmur of wind through the trees and the whispered *slap-slap* of the lake against the shore to hold back the lonely stillness. A sense of sorrowing loss brushed her.

I wonder if I will ever come back again.

"I left a key under the flagstone near the back door." She drew a deep, steadying breath. "Go there sometimes, if you want. Build a fire on my hearth. Try the organ, to see if the mice have been at the bellows again."

Jeff said, "I want you to telephone me—" and when she moved her head in mute negation, "—please. In a week or two, whenever you can tell me how things are going for you. I think I'm going to need to know. Will you?"

"I—yes. All right, I will. I promise."

They did not kiss, nor say good-bye. Their hands touched; then she turned away from him and went up the ramp and into the plane.

6.

Casey looked at what she had just finished typing: *Emotional Condition as Causative of Illness. 1. Explain briefly why the repression of anger or aggression may result in feelings of fear.* She switched off the typewriter and leaned back in her chair, arching her body to relieve the tension along her spine. "I'll bite, why does it?"

Jeff looked up from his paperwork. "Why does what?"

"Repression of anger or aggression result in feelings of fear?"

"Fear of punishment. As kids we were punished for being aggressive, or losing our temper, and as we grow older we try to hide it. It's a subconscious thought habit resulting in a behavioral pattern which often carries over into adult life."

Casey shrugged. "I guess it's simple when you know how. Thank you, Doctor."

"Anytime."

She left her chair and went to the window, to look down over the campus. The skies were leaden and rain had been falling steadily all day. It looked outside like she felt inside.

I suppose the assumption is if you know the psychological reason something is hurting you, it lessens the hurt. I doubt the hell out of that.

She may have made a small sound because Jeff glanced up again, more aware of her now. "Tired?"

"A little. We've been at it several hours without a break."

"How about breaking, then? I'm ready." He shoved the papers into a drawer. "Let's go to lunch."

She looked doubtfully at the sodden day and back at him. "If I eat at the union one more time this week I can do my own paper on Tarant College hamburger as a causative of food poisoning."

"Then we go into town—the Copper Kettle. I'll spring for it. Get your things. I'll bring my car around to the east portico so you can get out without being drenched." They smiled at each other and for a moment it was—almost—like old times, but she quickly denied herself hope. It was no good saying anything was the same now, and she may as well face it. The only time he had entered into a conversation with her about anything apart from work in the past few days had been when he wanted to talk to her about Maryanne Anderson, and her problem. She was losing Jeff, whatever part of him she had ever really had. It was there in his preoccupation, a withdrawal of himself from her. There had been a time when if he was in one of his moods for too long, she had her own ways of snapping him out of it. They were of no use to her now. Whatever they had had going for them, Jeff was obviously cooling it—or was he simply giving himself a cooling-out period from something else? How was she to know, and how long was she supposed to wait?

If he thinks I can slip back into the

employer-employee role as easily as I slipped out of it, he's off his trolley.

In the past few days she had tried to nurture a kind of cold anger against him so maybe the hurt would be less that way. He was not being fair. Honesty, even brutal honesty—*the truth is I just don't want you any longer, Casey*—that she could take. At least she thought she could take it, although she was finding out some surprising truths about herself. For one thing, she was a coward. One hell of a good way to get honesty, brutal or otherwise, was to come right out and ask him, "Do you want to call it quits?" but it was a plain case of no guts. She was scared to death of the answer.

At the Copper Kettle she sat with Jeff in a booth and they ate and talked small talk, and Casey decided unhappily it was not her imagination that there were moments when in a kind of abashed mutual understanding they avoided looking into each other's eyes.

After a time, Jeff said, "I feel guilty, asking you to work so much overtime. I haven't left us much leeway for getting caught up on loose ends before the winter session is in full swing. Keith Borlan is taking a six weeks' leave in December. His mother is terminally ill, back in Maine. I'll have to take over his chair. It's either that or leave his class to the tender mercies of Rolfe

Amboy, and my conscience won't let me do that. . . .

"Did I tell you the regents are meeting with the faculty Monday evening? That's only three days away and the final reports have to be ready. We'll have to manage somehow. Get someone in to help, if you need to."

"Don't worry about it. We'll manage."

"There'll be dinner at President Moore's home before the meeting. You're invited, if you're feeling social."

"I'll force myself. I've a new dress no one has seen; it's screaming red."

"You'd better take your car, otherwise you'll be stuck with the faculty wives while the meeting's in session, and that may go on for hours. You can leave whenever you want to, and I can take a cab back to my apartment after the meeting."

Casey sat quietly until this new wave of disappointment had rolled over her. After the last faculty dinner she and Jeff had slipped away to recap the evening over a few drinks and more than a few laughs. Then they had returned to her apartment together.

Forget it. You heard what the man said.

The evening of the dinner began with what seemed to Casey at least a mild promise. Jeff looked at her in her red dress and gave an appreciative whistle. "Hey now, that ought to make the faculty wives hate your insides." He handed her into her car as if she were royalty, and he drove, and she sat beside him in a vague pleasant glow which lasted precisely two minutes after they were inside President Moore's house.

Helene Amboy slithered up to them to say, "Megan, my dear, how marvelous you look. Doesn't she look marvelous, Doctor Kendall? And how *nice* to see you two back together again!"

There was no mistaking her meaning, not for Casey, who knew exactly what she meant; nor for Jeff, who knew, and who knew that Casey knew. He never stopped smiling but his quick glance at Casey held an awareness and his jaw got a white ridge along it.

Casey ate her dinner in a haze of misery and never knew what she had eaten. Directly afterward she made her excuses to the host and hostess and tried to slip away unnoticed, but Jeff intercepted her at the door.

"Please wait up for me. I think we'd better talk."

She nodded. "Yes, I expect we'd better."

It was only a little past ten when she let Jeff into the apartment. He came in and sat in his accustomed chair beside Casey's fake fireplace.

"The meeting was over early?"

"No, I made an excuse and cut out."

"Do you want a drink?"

"Yes, thanks."

She made them each one, brought him his, carried hers to the coffee table. She sat on the couch, looking at her drink without touching it. She made no attempt to break the little silence which had fallen.

It's your show, love, so you ring the curtain up, or down, or whatever comes next.

He said abruptly, "For someone who gets paid for his expertise on human behavior, I should take a salary cut. Obviously I've had my head in the sand."

"You're talking about what Helene said."

"I am. Do you want to tell me what you've heard?"

"What should I have heard?" She was appalled when a single large tear rolled down her face. She struck it angrily away with her fingers. Jeff shook his head.

"I'd rather you'd tell me."

"All right, I've heard talk, rather a lot of it. Most of it did come from Helene, but you may be certain she spread it around."

"Precisely what did she tell you?"

"Are you sure you want me to be precise?"

"Yes."

"She said you'd been having an affair with a married woman named Shane Manning, who happens to be the niece of a former Tarant seminary dean. I don't know just what that last has to do with it, but it did seem to add some sort of zest to the telling." She sipped at her drink, then meticulously wiped away a drop of moisture from the coffee table with a paper napkin. "If it's true, maybe you feel it comes under the heading of none of my business, only if it's true, I'd rather had heard it from you. And I'm afraid I do believe it, so tell me there's nothing to it and I'll do any penance you name."

He said after a long moment, "I'm afraid I can't tell you that."

"Yes. Well." She tried to smile, then her shoulders drooped and she exhaled a weary sigh. "I feel like there's a hole in my gut and a cold wind blowing through it."

"I'm feeling a little of that myself. I'm damned sorry you've been hurt. I doubt that helps much, but I want you to know I don't feel good about it."

"It doesn't help much, but thanks, all the same." She turned her head away and said something in a tone so muffled that it was all but inaudible. "She's better in bed than I am, right?"

"What? Oh, good God, Casey, don't put a cheap label on what you have been to me!"

"Faithful secretary." Her mouth twisted. "Great and good friend." Then she drew a steadying breath. "All right, are you going to tell me anything about her?"

"What do you want to know?"

"Nothing, really. I guess it's you I want to know about. Are you in love with her?"

His reply was indirect. "Someone said love is believing one woman is different from all the rest. Shane isn't that different from a thousand others. She's got a sackful of hang-ups; she can be very mature and childish as hell all in a breath. She's caught between the world she grew up in and the one she can't quite seem to grow up into; she's unhappily married and unhappy, period, mostly because she's been letting other people make her decisions all her life. She's talented and sweet and in some ways as naive as a schoolgirl—and yes, I guess I am in love with her."

So there you have it. Now what do you think?

Well, I think Doctor Jeffrey Kendall's rules on the love game are so much protective coloring, dig? I think, furthermore, that I've known it all along and accepting it has been a little old thing known as saving one's pride. Now the rule book has blown up in our faces and someone is going to get hurt, and guess who that someone is.

She looked consideringly at him. "You don't want to be in love with her, do you? What is it with you, Jeff? You care about people, but you don't want to care too much for any one person. Why? Do you think that would make you personally responsible for all those hang-ups you're so good at diagnosing?"

"Maybe you're a better psychologist than I am."

"Is she in love with you?"

He hesitated for a moment. "I honestly don't know. I think she is—in a way—but after all, she is married, and she has gone back to her husband."

"You didn't tell her you loved her."

It was not a question.

Jeff returned her look, silent for so long that she thought he was not going to reply, but at length he said, "No."

"Oh, wow!" She struck her forehead lightly with the heel of her hand. "You really blew it, didn't you? Rule number one, never say 'I love you.' Tell me, did you explain to her about marriage being an antiquated tribal custom?"

"Go ahead, I deserve it."

"No. You're hurting, and I'm the one who knows how much. So now what?"

"Now nothing, probably. She's gone. I did ask her to telephone me, but I've a feeling she won't. If I had asked her to stay, I think she might have, but—" He shrugged and did not finish.

"You know something, Jeff? People like us, I

don't think we're really very bright. We make a big thing of tossing all the rules out the window, and wouldn't it be funny if they weren't meant to *rule* us at all, but only to protect us against ourselves? So—where does it go from here?"

"Nowhere, I'd imagine. I'll just have to get over it. It'll take a little time, that's all."

"And where do *I* go from here?"

He shook his head. "That's up to you."

She was quiet for a time, then:

"I'm not going anywhere, not for a while. I don't have all that much pride left to save. But I'll tell you something, Jeff, I'm tired of playing the game, and I'm up to *here* with the rules. I'd as soon break number one right now and say I love you. I do, you know."

He nodded, silent, not looking at her now.

"I'm just bloody optimist enough to believe that if I give it my best shot, you might love me, too. So—I'll wait for you to get over her. I don't know how long I'll wait, but at least until I'm certain there's no real chance of our ever getting to really know each other."

That seemed to surprise him. "I'd say we know each other pretty well."

"I wouldn't. Physically, maybe, but there's more to it than that, isn't there? You don't really know anything about me, any more than I know what you're really like inside. There have been things I sensed in you, troubled things that I wanted to be able to share, and didn't dare ask about, like the night here when you had just come back from burying your father. There was something about you, something more than just the grief of losing someone you loved. It was almost as if you were *afraid—*"

"Fear of defeat," he said strangely, and she echoed it.

"Defeat? I don't understand. Do you want to tell me?"

He got up and came to sit beside her on the couch, leaning back and closing his eyes with a sigh of weariness. "I told you once, I have my hang-ups, just like anyone. There's a fear that comes when someone you love dies and you're faced with the prospect of living with the knowledge that you may have failed him."

"You're talking about your father?"

"Yes. Not even Uncle Francis knows the whole story. My father died in an alcoholic ward, raving in delirium, calling for someone, they said—for me, maybe. I don't know. I wasn't there."

She said, presently, "So that's it—your concern with that sort of thing. All those kids, and the hotline—"

"It isn't a transference, I know better than that. Call it a compensation, if you like. When I was fifteen we watched my mother die, dad and

I—a grim kind of death. It was one of those swift, deadly nerve things, and before the end she was a prisoner in her own body, with everything dying except her mind. Fully conscious and aware, unable to communicate except by blinking her eyes, and that look in them that seemed to be saying *Help me*. It destroyed my father. He took longer dying, that's all. He'd never been a heavy drinker but it began after mother died, and within a year he was a hopeless alcoholic. He'd straighten himself out for a while and then he'd be back at it again.

"I knew he was worse when I was away at college, so summers I'd spend all the time with him that I could, trying to help. I know what the good reverends at the seminary would say about weakness and defiance of God's will, and all that crap—The plain fact was that he had loved my mother deeply, and he couldn't live with what had happened to her. I didn't understand enough about what was happening to him to be much help. He had money, so there was no pressing economic situation, but there were some bad times when I felt I was going to have to stick it out with him for as long as he was alive, and it made for a pretty bleak future. I resented it, and I guess sometimes I hated him, but I'd bury the feeling and try all the harder to help. I think he was ahead of me there; he finally let me know he had no intention of my wasting my life trying to hold his together. It got so if I came home with the idea of staying any length of time, he'd leave. Sometimes he was gone for weeks at a time and I had no idea where to even begin to look for him.

"I finally had to give it up. I came to the States for my postgrad work. I taught for a while in a college back East and I began doing a lot of research into alcoholism. I came out here one summer to see Uncle Francis. I hadn't seen him in years; his health made it impossible for him to come up to us. Anyway, I liked it here and when Uncle Francis heard there was a department opening at Tarant, he got in touch.

"That's about all there is to it. Tarant is a long way from Quebec, and after I came here I saw dad only twice. One of those times he was in a drying-out place. He looked like hell—skin and bones, all burned out—but he seemed glad to see me. I suppose I'd never really given up hope that something would happen—the miracle—then I could bring him to spend the rest of his days with me. He never had any intention of that happening, of course. It wasn't easy, going back to put him away, remembering what it used to be like when my mother was alive and the three of us were together. Anyway, I came back from Canada and you were here and you held me together. That makes you special to me, and I've repaid you badly."

He stopped talking then, and she asked, "Have you given any thought to what effect the gossip might have on your position here? It's a small school, and there are people here to whom you haven't always endeared yourself."

Jeff shrugged. "Shane is gone, and they can only conjecture. When she doesn't come back— One nice thing about gossips, they usually have a short attention span. Something else will come along for them to get their teeth into. I'm not worried about that part of it."

"Well, if you don't mind, I think I'll worry a little about it."

"I hate it that I've exposed you to their clacking tongues."

"Don't sweat it." She smiled faintly. "At least while they're talking about me they're letting someone else alone, right?"

At least I understand him a little better now. He just wasn't going to love anyone, not the way his father loved his mother, not the way he loved his father, either, with that terrible feeling of responsibility. I think there are some areas in which Jeff hasn't ever quite grown up, either.

What is it, anyhow, to grow up? I wonder if any of us ever really do?

Presently she said musingly, "Once upon a time you said to me that you thought a lot of psychologists aren't able to handle their own hang-ups—and I thought you were kidding!"

He leaned forward to take her face between his hands and kiss her lightly. "I'm going home. I'm going to sleep, and try not to have bad dreams about how I've screwed everything up. You get some rest, too."

She promised, "I will," but when he had gone she sat for a long while, alone and feeling the aloneness keenly.

Understanding him a little better only makes me love him more, and I'm not sure that's good.

At least, she had had the guts to say *I love you*, an act of honesty which made her stand taller in her own sight, and that was good, wasn't it?

7.

On the flight home Shane reviewed the events of the past few months dispassionately, caught up for the time being in a sort of vacuum, feeling nothing clearly but knowing a time must come when painful and conflicting emotions would be thrust upon her. There would be no one to turn to then, to help her reason things out; so she must meet them, sort them, survive them alone.

She wondered if Jeff Kendall had ever guessed at the complete emotional collapse which had threatened her when she first came to Shadow Lake. A vacation alone—that was what David Price had prescribed. He had a notion, he said, that her cottage and the lake might prove to be stronger medicine than anything he could prescribe from a pharmacy.

It turned out to be strong medicine, that prescription, and it had side effects. David might be shocked if he knew.

She could not really say when it had begun, the depression, the fatigue. She had been tired all the time, arising in the morning as exhausted as when she went to bed, with barely the energy to drag through the day. It was not really illness, only the relentless weariness, the irritability against which she must battle, the tension which made the least of unexpected noises thrill along her jangled nerves like chalk down a blackboard. She had no appetite and there was a lump in her throat as if she had swallowed something that would not go down.

Toward the end there had been a bad quarrel with Court. She no longer recalled what had triggered it, but they had carried the quarrel to their bed and it died out in stubborn withdrawal into silence, into sleep which came slowly to both of them.

There had been a time when they had lived up to a youthful pact never to sleep with a quarrel unresolved between them. When was that, a thousand years ago? This had been a quarrel made more bitter by her dim awareness that the seeds of truth were in Court's indictment.

"When did I ever do anything that really pleased you, Shane? Either it's been one hell of a long time or you've been careful not to let me know about it. Half the time I think you can't stand the sight of me anymore, let alone have me lay a hand on you."

In these moments when he drove at her with unkind words born of his own frustration, she was torn by guilt because she rarely felt any desire for Court now, and long ago it had become too tiresome to pretend. She always gave herself to him without protest, but he was not deceived and it made a silent but deep conflict too often reflected in what should have been only miniarguments.

Finally one morning she arose to dress and looked at Court, still sleeping. He was snoring gently, making small sighing sounds as he breathed in and out. He looked ridiculous and somehow terribly vulnerable. She was painfully torn between guilt, and unreasoning anger.

I've got to leave him. I can't endure it for one more day.

It was insane. A rational, responsible wife didn't just walk out like that.

Was your husband cruel to you, Mrs. Manning?

Not intentionally. Court is basically a kind person.

Unfaithful?

Never. I'm certain of it.

He has provided well for you?

Extremely well. He's very proud of being able to buy me almost anything I might want.

Then why do you no longer wish to live with him?

I'm not happy—more than just not happy, I'm wretched. I want to be alone, to be free, to be myself, whatever that is. I think I was always most nearly myself when I was alone.

Not to have to try anymore, isn't that what you want?

Yes. *Yes.*

Court made waking sounds. He rolled over and lifted himself to an elbow. "What time is it?"

"Past seven. I'm going in to start breakfast now." Unconsciously she put a hand to her forehead.

He asked, "Head aching again?"

"A little. I'll take aspirin."

The headaches had grown worse, and the weariness. Mornings she went mechanically about the business of preparing breakfast, wanting only to get Court out of the house so she could be alone, sink into a chair, and rest. She grew thin and her eyes were shadowed. Dee Andreas, her neighbor, fretted about her.

"Honestly, Shane, you look like cold death warmed over! You ought to get a checkup."

"I'm fine—a little run-down, that's all."

It was more than that, she knew. She was fed up to the teeth with the meaningless treadmill of daily existence with Court, with going to bed with Court.

I don't enjoy it and I can't make babies, so why bother?

The truth was, she suspected, that she had grown totally unable to cope with life. So many things frightened her and she was filled with vague, undefined apprehensions. She was terrified of the whole world and what was happening to it. It was as if she were a solitary alien among creatures she could neither recognize nor relate to. Whenever she could, she avoided the television newscasts to which Court was addicted, but now and again tidings of the world about her were thrust at her and she was sickened by what she heard. The country was full of something unhealthy; it was on the air, in the talk one heard—the cynicism of four-letter words and pat, meaningless phrases—and in the very air one breathed. Corruption in high places and the crime rate climbing and pornography and rutting loveless men and women and mass murders and race problems and defeating clergymen.... God is dead. One night as Court sat watching the news she raged at him, "For the love of heaven, turn that thing *off!*" and as he stared after her, agape, she fled into the bathroom and threw up.

Sometimes, only once in a very long while, she tried to pray, but even if she had been certain to whom or what she prayed, she did not know what to ask for. She could only say despairingly, "Please."

She considered suicide, with calm logic. One would need to be clever. It must look an accident. Suicide was cruel to those who were left behind, and she must not be cruel to Court. Nothing so brutal as blowing her brains out.

An electrical appliance toppling into the water while she was bathing—

The insanity of it repelled her. Please—

It was Court who finally persuaded her to see a doctor. If he hoped there was some medication which might improve her disposition he did not say as much. She gave in, too apathetic to protest, and went back to David Price, the wonderfully blunt, kind man, who had been her personal physician during the earlier years of her marriage.

During the examination he asked her a series of seemingly irrelevant questions.

How was Court?

Court was fine. Working too hard, but then, you know Court.

How did she like living in Regency? Was she taking on too many social obligations?

A few, more than she was up to, really, but people kept after her. Lately she'd been turning them all down because she didn't feel like putting forth the effort.

Headaches?

Yes, frequently.

Any trouble sleeping?

Sometimes, although it was not so much that. No matter how long she slept she never seemed to awaken feeling rested. David might think it idiotic but she was nervy and often had a feeling of apprehension as if at any moment something dreadful was going to happen.

At this point in the interview the tears came without warning. She was horrified, but she could not stop. She sat there blubbering and David waited in patient silence.

When she was quiet again, he asked, "Shane, how long since you've taken a real vacation?"

"Two years, three—I don't know. Court isn't

able to get away very often; anyway he feels he isn't." She dabbed childishly at her flushed, tearstained face. "We did go back to Shadow Lake one summer. I still have a cottage there. It belonged to my family."

"You like it there?"

"Yes. It's quiet and peaceful, and very beautiful. Court doesn't like to go there."

"Tell me, have you ever taken a vacation without Court?"

"No. Why on earth should I?"

"Why on earth shouldn't you? Frankly, Shane, I can't find very much wrong with you—"

"And you're going to tell me it's just nerves."

You see, Court, I didn't need a thirty-dollar office call to tell me that. I've a touch of soul sickness, that's all, and there's not a pill or a shot that can do anything for it.

David snapped at her, "Are you the doctor or am I? I'm not going to tell you it's 'just' anything. The truth is, you're suffering a near-clinical depression that could get a lot worse before it gets better." Then at her frightened look he softened his tone. "It's not uncommon, in these pressure times, although I do see it more often in men."

"I don't understand. Near-clinical—what is that? What if it were clinical?"

"There are drugs, therapy—sometimes we're

obliged to go to shock treatment."

A little jolt of anger brought her upright in her chair. "Isn't that what you're trying now, David, a little shock treatment of your own?"

"Come off it, Shane. I want you to take that chip off your shoulder, put it between your teeth, and listen to me. You must have recognized the danger signals yourself or you wouldn't be here. I could give you tranquilizers, but they would only mask the symptoms, if they did anything at all. Sometimes they even intensify the symptoms. For the time being, my prescription would be that you get away by yourself for a long rest. By yourself—do you understand me? Go to your lake for a few weeks—as long as you can. Then we'll see."

"What are you trying to say?"

"Damn it, I'm saying it! I want to help you, but you're going to have to help yourself, too."

"Are you quite certain it isn't a psychiatrist I need?" She meant it for sarcasm but he replied, calmly:

"No, I'm not certain, but I'm not recommending it just yet. I think you still have an option."

"David," suddenly she was trying not to cry again, "either I'm being terribly stupid or you aren't spelling it out for me. What's wrong with me?"

"Sometimes it's called neurotic fatigue. I daresay one could compare it to battle fatigue in combat men."

"I see. And may I ask what causes this—this neurosis?"

He sighed. "Dear God, send me just one female who doesn't turn to ice at the very mention of that word."

"That's very amusing, David, but it doesn't clarify anything."

"All right, I can't tell you precisely what's causing your trouble although I've noticed that usually the largest contributing factor is a thing known unclinically as unhappiness. I've known you for—what, seven, eight years? You first came to me because you were troubled over your inability to conceive. After considerable treatment you did get pregnant but they were difficult pregnancies, and there was the trauma of the two stillbirths. Obviously you aren't pregnant now. Are you still trying?"

"No." Her voice hardened. "I've given it up." I could tell you a sad story about that but I'm not going to tell it to anyone. Not to you and not to any psychiatrist.

"I know how badly you wanted children but there are women for whom childbearing is just too dangerous. I'm afraid you're one of those."

"You told Court that, of course."

He looked puzzled, then shrugged. "I don't

recall. I probably did. Why?"

"Nothing. It's of no importance." Only that it did make such a fine, noble excuse.

"You haven't considered adopting?"

"No." A man who doesn't want children of his own isn't apt to want anyone else's. I would. I'd take any child—black, white, brown, red. I'd be happy and proud if I could make a child's world a little better, and justify my existence in my own.

After a moment she said, "I'm behaving badly. I'm sorry, David. Please go on."

"This type of depression, unfortunately, seems to be becoming more common. Women react to it in different ways, just as men do. They may tend to become hypochondriac, or severely withdrawn; they may take to drinking—"

Or they may contemplate suicide?

"Or they may carry on and hope for the difficulty to right itself. Unfortunately, it seldom does, unless the cause is righted, too. I'm counting on your ability to face your own problem and decide what you must do about it—and for the love of heaven use your good judgment and common sense. Just because I haven't pinpointed some physical ailment and prescribed for it, don't go away thinking I've turned into some kind of crank. Frankly, in your case I suspect all a psychiatrist could do would be to try to help you figure out what your problem is, and somehow I've an idea you already know."

Left to her own devices she might have ignored his prescription but without her knowledge David telephoned Court, who promptly demanded, "Why didn't you tell me what David Price said?"

"Because there's nothing wrong with me but nerves, although I'm not having a nervous breakdown, if that's what's worrying you."

"What's worrying me is seeing you the way you are, so tired and edgy. I don't have to be a doctor to know you could end up with some very real physical illness."

She was irritable. "Court, I don't want to talk about it. I'm not going and that's the end of it."

The end of it had been that she did go, of course—reluctant, doubting the wisdom of it. Hadn't she read or heard that the only place to come to grips with a problem is where the problem is?

Won't it be a fine joke on David and Court if it turns out it's only myself I can't cope with, and I really go off the deep end, up there alone.

She made the three-hour flight, leaving the plane at Tarant and boarding a bus for the thirty-mile trip up the mountain to Shadow Lake. As the aged vehicle lumbered along, engine complaining loudly at the steep grade, she looked about her at the beautiful, well-remembered country, and drew a deep slow breath, feeling a sense of release and a beginning gladness that she had come.

The driver unloaded her luggage in the village, in front of a frame structure bearing the legend *Bus Depot*. In one window a sign said *Open* and on the locked front door a card announced *Closed for lunch*. The whole village, she thought amusedly, must be closed for lunch because on the quiet narrow streets no one and nothing moved.

She stood looking about her. So small was the basin cradling the hamlet that the little roads seemed to slant sharply upward and disappear into the forest. Above, the cragged peaks loomed darkly against the sky.

A vehicle of dubious vintage with *Taxi* handlettered across its side stood at the curb, an old man drowsing at the wheel. Shane approached him and he lifted his head as she spoke to him.

"Howdy, ma'am." He gave her a gap-toothed grin. "Restin' my eyes a spell and that old bus must've sneaked right past me. Can I take you somewheres?"

"Do you know the Parker cottage?"

"Been knowin' it thirty year, more or less. Nobody there."

"I know. It belongs to me."

"That so?" Interest sparked his glance.

"Thought I ought to know you. You're Miz Grace Parker's niece. Used to summer here."

He opened the door and climbed out, stowed her bags and easel into the rear seat. "You best to set up front with me. Busted spring back there. Good enough for flatlanders but you're more like home folks. Say, your place been closed up quite a spell. Apt to be purty musty and dusty. If you was to need a hand to help you tidy, my old woman's right smart at housework. Charge you reasonable, too."

"Thank you. I'll bear it in mind, Mr.—"

"Call me Sam. Ever'body does. No reason you should remember me, Miz Parker. I'm easy to forget, like the feller says."

"I'm Mrs. Manning now."

"That right? You marry a local boy?"

"He lived in Tarant. I doubt you'd know him."

"Likely not. I don't mix much with them town folks. Most of 'em is too high livin' for my taste."

Shane stifled a little laugh. No definition she had ever heard for high living would fit the Tarant people she had known.

They left the village and took the narrow winding road which skirted the lake. The Parker cottage lay a considerable distance from the village in an isolated area. Shane feasted her eyes on the glow of aspen and birch against the somber eternal green of the pines. Along the road chinquapin scrub showed its bursting burrs with the glossy nuts inside, and beyond it the slopes were turning vivid with early autumn hues of goldenrod, goneaway, and sumac.

A nameless yearning flared through her. Maybe I can find a new beginning here, she thought wistfully. To have felt that I wanted to be all through with living at twenty-eight—that *was* insane!

She would rest, the way David wanted, and she would steep herself in all the natural beauty that had faded to a dim memory in the frightening scurry of a sprawling California city. Maybe she could release, once and for all, the little lost dreams that had never come true.

Please.

They were going along the lake now, placid and silvery in the midday sun. Cottages, deserted and silent for the most part, were scattered along the shore. There was as yet little about Shadow Lake which was commercial and most of the cottages, she imagined, would still be owned by Tarant people.

As if he picked up on her thoughts the old man vouchsafed, "'Bout the same as it allus was. Been some talk about puttin' a state scenic highway through this way up to Comber's Ridge and out t'other way to Riverton—a kind of loop.

Reckon we'd have tourists comin' out of our ears, then. Some Tarant folks rents out their places to strangers, fishermen and suchlike. I don't cotton much to flatlanders myself. They ain't a friendly lot for the most part, and they want a sight more service than they rightly got a call to expect, seein' how little they want to pay. Things'll change, all right, but I hate to see it come."

They rattled to a stop before a rambling log structure in the shade of towering pines. Shane got out and walked along the winding flagstone path, the old man following. She moved ankle deep through dead leaves on the terrace and taking a key from her purse she let herself into the long windowed gallery which lay along the entire front of the building. With a sigh of pure pleasure she stood looking about her. The logs which formed the walls and the overhead beams had been smoothed and sanded to a high luster. Windows with deep padded sills opened outward, overlooking the terraced yard and the lake. She moved about, opening windows, letting in the pleasantly lonely sound of pines, the murmur of waves against the lakeshore. Sam struggled in with her luggage.

Court had wired the utilities people and the power had been turned on. In the kitchen, Shane switched on the refrigerator. Behind her, Sam said, "Evenin's is nippy now, and you'll likely want a fire. I could fetch you some wood."

"Yes, please do that."

"You'll be needin' supplies, too. I could come back and fetch you in to the village, if you want. Tradin' post closes at six this time of year."

"Just a few things will do me for tonight. Maybe I could give you a list and you could bring them out to me."

"Yes, ma'am. Bein's you're here without no car, best I check in on you now and ag'in. No charge to you, you unnerstand, unless you was to want me to drive you somewheres."

Shane smiled at him. "Thank you. I expect I'll be calling on you. I live in California, you see, and my husband felt it was too far for me to drive my car, alone, so I flew. It's good to know there's transportation available."

"Anytime, ma'am. Bein' you ain't got a telephone, neither, you can do like some other folks does, put up a mail flag on the road yonder and put a note in the box. Mailman'll see I get the message. He's allus back in the village by noon."

"Thank you. That's very convenient."

He gave her his wide grin. "Well, us villagers got some ways of doin' a sight more neighborly than any city I ever seen. I'll be back with your things later, if you'll just give me a list."

She complied and he touched his cap and went

away, humming tunelessly.

Shane pulled a dustcover from a couch on the gallery and lay down to rest, although despite the long flight and the jolting trip by bus she was not really tired. It was the excitement of being back, she told herself. She listened to the quiet talk of pines and the murmur of water, and was brushed by the feeling that once more she had escaped to sanctuary here.

After a time, she slept.

She awakened to the sound of Sam's return. He had brought her supplies, a box of kindling and several fire logs.

"Plenty of downed trees in your stand above here. I could come back tomorrow and split up a pile to do you a spell."

"Yes, thank you, that would be fine."

She fixed herself a sketchy supper of cold cuts, and made up a fresh bed. Then she went out onto the gallery. Sitting in a deep old swing, she watched the day die over the lake. The city, and Court, seemed very far away.

Footsteps came along the path and a man paused at the terrace steps. She could see him dimly in the dying light. He was a thin middle-aged man with a thatch of gray hair falling across a high forehead. He was clad in casual attire but a clerical collar revealed his calling. Although he seemed vaguely familiar to her, Shane could find no place for him in her memory.

"Good evening. I'm Father Francis Doheny. I hope you won't think I'm intruding, but I've a cottage across the cove and out here we rather keep an eye out for each other's places."

"I'm glad to hear it. I'm not a burglar; I'm Shane Manning and this place belongs to me. Won't you come in and visit for a little?"

"Thank you." He came into the gallery and took the chair she offered. "Shane Parker—of course. I knew your father well, and I had met your uncle although he and I were not really acquainted."

I'll just bet you weren't. To Uncle Gregory, all Catholics were the devil's advocates.

"I remember you as a young girl. I'd see you ride past on your bicycle, and once in a while you'd stop and talk. I fixed a tire for you one day."

"Oh, yes, now I remember! I felt I should know you, but it has been rather a long time."

"Have you your family with you?"

"I'm here alone. My husband couldn't leave his business. I've been a bit under the weather and my doctor thought the change might be good for me. It is wonderful, being back."

"Well, I'm on a rather enforced holiday myself—had some surgery, one thing and another. It makes a fine excuse for getting my fill of fishing.

Do you fish, Mrs. Manning? Or may I call you Shane? I used to."

"Please do. No, I never got the hang of it, but I may try, while I'm here. I'm sure there's some old tackle about somewhere."

"We've much more than we need at my place, and we can fix you up with whatever's lacking. A nephew of mine, Doctor Kendall—Jeffrey, his name is—is here with me a great deal of the time just now. He's head of the psychology department at Tarant, although at present he's supposed to be here finishing a book. Like me, he spends a great deal of his time on the water—thinking, he claims. I've an idea I'm setting him a bad example."

"Kendall—should I know the name?"

"Oh, no, he came here only four years ago. Young chap, early thirties. His mother was my only sister. She married a Canadian and he took her to Quebec to live. So you see, I've not had a family of my own for too long. Until he came here to Tarant I'd seen very little of Jeffrey."

"Well, I'm sure it's very nice for you that he's here. May I offer you something, Father? Coffee?"

"Thank you, no. I must be getting back. My bedtime is quite early—my doctors are stuffy about that."

"It was good of you to come by."

"If we can be of assistance, please call on us. I'll volunteer my nephew if you need lifting or fixing—younger and stronger, you know. Perhaps I can help you with your fishing. I'm really pretty knowledgeable, although Jeffrey is a purist when it comes to casting, and he's not a particular admirer of my technique."

Shane laughed. "Then I think I'll avoid him. From what I do remember about it, I was always lucky just to get the line in the water, any old way!"

As she lay in her solitary bed that night, it occurred to her that it was a relief not to have Court snoring beside her. Then, perversely, she was saddened by the thought.

Can this marriage be saved—?

That was the sort of thing the women's magazines loved to play around with. Idly she wondered if anyone had ever done "*Should* this marriage be saved?" When two people were simply not good together—

She had thought she and Court were good together at first, although their points of difference had been clear from the outset. She had never considered herself foolishly romantic, but there had been secret longings. Probably every young girl had them. There had been disappointments. As a lover, Court had not been all tenderness and understanding, perhaps because he was too young and inexperienced himself to understand her needs. He was abrupt and demanding, often taking injured offense when she was slow in responding or unable to respond at all. Yet when she made tentative attempts to talk it over with him, he would grow red with embarrassment and anger. At length she began to guess at the obscure shame in him. To Court, sex was just something you did, not a thing you talked about.

Court was inclined to be dictatorial and Shane's childhood submissiveness had left her poorly equipped to resist domination, even when the first warm glow of *belonging* had faded and she had chafed a bit at times under Court's assertiveness. Sometimes in those latter days she had looked into the mirror and fancied she could see a physical resemblance to Aunt Grace, who had been no blood kin to her.

On the other side of the coin, Court was generous with her, always, and solicitous of her welfare. Too solicitous, Shane had come to feel, with the same imperious concern he had shown for his mother.

If, in those earlier days, Shane had not been ready to admit that the marriage had been a mistake, still she sometimes thought the tragedy of Court's mother had been too recent; they were reacting too sharply. They should have waited.

New disappointment had come with her gradual realization that Court did not really want children. The plain truth was that he did not need them. Shane wanted them, needed them to fulfill her as a woman, to care for and love, to build about her the family for which she had yearned as long as she could remember.

She had not permitted herself to worry unduly about it. If having children meant so much to her, Court conceded grudgingly, then it might be all right to have one or two—later, when they could afford it. She thought that having children as a concession to someone else was a poor reason. But he would feel differently when he had a child of his own; she was certain of it.

When they had begun to prosper and could afford to start their family, she had found herself unable to conceive, and that was when she had gone to David Price for the first time. There were painful treatments, corrective surgery, the uncertainty of waiting—the joy when at length she did become pregnant. The joy was somewhat unilateral, with Court being less than enthusiastic about it. She refused to let it dampen her excitement.

The child was born dead in her seventh month of pregnancy.

Some congenital weakness in her, David said. More treatment, more time...

The second pregnancy was more difficult. She was desperately ill much of the time and a worried Court said, "Honey, you mustn't let yourself care so much."

It angered her. "But I do care. My baby is going to live!"

Her baby was stillborn in the eighth month. He nearly took his mother with him in death and for an agonized while she wished that he had. David told her sternly that now she must wait for a longer time—two years, three—and she must not build her hopes too high.

She flung at him, "I'll wait, but understand me, David—I am going to try again!"

Her strength returned only slowly but with it reason came. She could see clearly now that she had made her second attempt too soon after losing the first baby. What was needed was a little common sense and patience. She must wait until she herself was certain. All of this she explained carefully to Court.

"I'll know," she said confidently. "I'm sure it's what went wrong before. I was rushing things and I was too anxious, like you said. In the future I'll be wiser about it."

For some time Court had been bothered by a small growth beneath one shoulder blade. His clothing, particularly his heavier winter shirts, rubbed it and irritated. He had it checked at a small clinic near the plant.

"I think I'll have it taken off," he told Shane. "They say it isn't anything serious but it could cause me trouble sometime. I may as well do it, I suppose—darn thing is getting to be a nuisance."

"I think that's wise, only I wish you had gone to David Price."

"Well, the clinic is a good one and close to the office, so I went there. It's not all that big a deal."

Shane was disturbed to learn that they would keep him at the clinic overnight. "Just to remove a little growth?"

"It's only a routine precaution against infection. Probably lets them collect a bigger fee, too. Don't worry about it."

He would go into the clinic late one afternoon, he would be at home the next morning—and no, she was not to come to the clinic with him nor visit him in the evening.

"What for, for Pete's sake? I'll be home in less than twenty-four hours. Look, honey, don't build it into a federal case. You stay right here and take care of yourself. You're trying to get your own health back and I don't want you out driving in night traffic when there is no need for it."

Afterward she reflected that Court was so accustomed to her doing what he wanted that it would not have occurred to him she might disobey him this time; but when he had gone, nagging fear beset her. *Malignancy*—the dire word kept drifting through her mind until she panicked, certain Court was keeping something from her.

In early evening she dressed, called a cab (at least Court couldn't fuss at her for driving her car), and directed the driver to the clinic.

At the reception desk she asked for Court. The nurse said, "I've just come on duty. I'll have to find out from one of the doctors."

She spoke briefly on a house phone and presently a young man in a white jacket joined them.

"Doctor Fales, this lady is asking about her husband."

"Courtney Manning," Shane said, anxiously.

"Yes, he's my patient. I'll show you his room—"

"Well, of course I want to see him, but I was hoping to speak with you first. He's had the surgery?"

"Oh, yes, hours ago."

"And he's all right? I mean—"

"Perfectly all right." He was looking curiously at her. "I'm sorry if you've been worried, Mrs. Manning. Didn't your husband explain the procedure to you? Nothing to it, really—a vasectomy is one of the simplest of surgeries."

8.

"I'll never forgive you, Court, never! You had no right—"

Because her white-faced implacable fury frightened him, he grew angry, too.

"I had every damned bit as much right as you have to kill yourself trying to have a baby!" He put his hand on her arm, but she struck it furiously away.

"Don't touch me!"

He let his hand fall heavily to his side. "All right, get it out of your system, and then maybe you'll be able to listen to reason."

At the clinic, when the enormity of what the doctor was saying had gotten through to her, Shane had stared wordlessly at him for a moment, then she turned and went toward the doorway, hearing the doctor call, puzzledly, "But Mrs. Manning, don't you want to see your husband?" and not answering him.

They had not told Court of Shane's visit until morning, and he had hurried home then, bursting into the house, calling her. She refused to answer him but made him search her out. In their bedroom he stood in the doorway looking uncertainly at her.

"The doctor told me you were there last night and what he said to you. Shane, I didn't intend for you to find out like that, you know I didn't."

She made no reply but returned his gaze with a kind of cool contempt, until he resorted to bluster to mask his uneasiness. "As long as you just had to come to the clinic, why didn't you come on to the room, instead of tearing off like that?"

"Why should I have? We had nothing to talk about—or did you want to tell me some new lie?"

"It wasn't a lie. I did have the growth removed." The absurdity of his own defense embarrassed him and he reddened. "Shane, I didn't like having to lie to you. I would have told you later."

"Would you? Or would you just have let me go on trying, letting me believe you were just pouring your seed into a poor, cracked vessel?"

"For God's sake, I would have told you! You said yourself you were going to wait for a while this time, and I thought there was no point in your knowing unless you decided to try again."

"Then why couldn't you have waited?"

"Because accidents happen, that's why! I watched you nearly die once. I didn't want to see you take the chance again."

"So you took matters into your own hands and decided what was best for me, without giving me a choice, or even talking it over with me."

"All right, maybe I was wrong to go about it the way I did. I can't argue the point. But I'd made up my mind you weren't going through it again."

"You've made up your mind about a lot of things, haven't you?" She stared coldly at him. "Suppose you had wanted children as badly as I did? That would take a great deal of supposing, because you never did, we both know that—but try. Then would you have been so unwilling for me to try?"

"You aren't being fair."

Bitterly, she retorted, "Oh, look who's talking about being *fair!*"

Court shrugged in defeat. "You're just not going to try to see my side of it, are you? I don't think we'd better try to talk about it anymore, just now."

They had never talked about it again. There was nothing more to be said. The time had even come when Shane had tried to understand, and to forgive him, but it was no good. It did not occur to her then to leave him, but she went through a period of hating to have him touch her. She did not tell him that the times she had been able to respond to him most completely had been those when she was deeply aroused by the awareness that he might be making her pregnant. Now her burning resentment against him made his lovemaking unwelcome.

Nothing had been any good after that. With time she had adjusted somewhat, had been able to pull herself together and to resume the routine of their daily life, but the marriage had gone sour and both of them knew it.

In all honesty, she thought, Court had gone on

trying even after she had given up.

Our lovely new Regency home was for me. Everything he has ever done has been for me, in a sense—and I am sick to death of it all!

Now, alone in a place where she had spent so many hours alone as a child, Shane cried herself to sleep. She slept until nearly noon of the next day, and awakened feeling curiously calm and refreshed.

The September season at Shadow Lake was glorious, the nights autumn crisp, coolness lingering all through the day in places where the shadows lay deep. It was quiet, summer done with. Only a few stragglers, fishermen for the most part, were staying at the inn, and only a few of the cottages scattered along the shore were occupied now.

For the first few days Shane saw no one but old Sam, and she revelled in the solitude. Most of the supplies she needed were obtainable at the trading post, and if she wanted anything from Tarant she could send for it by the obliging bus driver who made the daily trip down in early morning, back at noon.

Several times she began a letter to Court, but there seemed little to say. She had wired him, from Tarant airport, of her safe arrival. Beyond that there was nothing to talk about except the lake. Court did not like to come here, and he had been a bit put out at her insistence on keeping the cottage, saying all it amounted to was taxes and upkeep, on a place too far away to get any good out of it.

In this matter she had been unaccustomedly adamant. It had been her haven in childhood, and even now that she was grown there was comfort in simply knowing it was still hers. To Court it was only an unwanted tie to a world he had left behind him, but Shane did not yield.

She sent him a postcard, bearing an uninspired photo of Shadow Lake trading post.

> There's not much to write. I'm sure you recall this isn't the most active place in the world. I'm comfortably settled in and feeling more rested. I hope everything is going nicely at home and that you are well. Give my best to Dee Andreas when you see her. Love, Shane.

As she was posting it she thought, appalled, I am fine and hope you are the same. Ten years of marriage and that is all I have to say to the man.

She ate when she was hungry, slept when she felt like it. She set up her easel in the north bedroom and worked now and then at a half-completed painting she had brought from home. When inactivity palled she wandered about, seeking out the secret places she had known as a child.

She enjoyed the old cottage, now that she had it cleaned and polished up. On a rainy afternoon she spent delightful hours drowsing before the fire she kindled in the mellow old stone fireplace, with its three-legged crane, the enormous andirons surmounted by ferocious-looking dog heads which had fascinated her as a child.

Many of the things in this room had been her Grandmother Parker's. The leather-covered box couch, the square mahogany library table with heavy carved legs and eagles' claws holding the glass rollers. She found a green-checked tablecloth in a linen chest, thinking in delight, I remember that, I fringed and knotted the edges myself when I was just a little thing. It was Grandmother's way of keeping me out of mischief.

She covered the table with the cloth, placed on it a copper bowl filled with autumn leaves, and was enchanted with the quiet glow it made in its corner of the room.

Grandmother's pump organ, massive and ornately scrolled, sat against one wall. When Shane tried it, tentatively, it emitted no sound. Tugging and shoving, she managed to get the instrument far enough from the wall to enable her to crawl behind it and investigate its innards. Mice, she discovered, had eaten holes in the bellows. She set about making patches with oilcloth and glue, deriding herself, expecting nothing for her pains; but when at length the repairs were complete and she stood before the thing, to pump vigorously with one foot, and press upon the keys—wheezy, lugubrious, soul-satisfying sound!

She sat and pumped and played until her fingers ached and her ankles sent out a strike call. She had an elated sense of achievement which she cheerfully admitted to herself was crazy, but it was almost as if she had built the instrument herself.

Now and then she toyed with the idea of journeying down to Tarant to seek out old acquaintances, but she decided she would have little in common with what few might be left. Then one day, on an impulse, she did accept old Sam's invitation to journey down the mountain.

"Me and the missus," he told her, "are goin' in to spend the afternoon with our married daughter. Be back in early evenin'—if you was a mind to go in and do some shoppin' or anythin'—"

"You could drop me off at the college; I think I might enjoy browsing around for awhile. I went to school there, you know."

There had been a few physical changes on the

campus. Shane walked slowly beneath autumn-bright trees, looking at the familiar old brick buildings, many of them wearing ancient cloaks of climbing ivy. There was a new building or two—a library, an angular, functionally modern building looking a bit arrogant and out of place among its senior-citizen neighbors. There were more students and certainly they had changed, she noted with mild amusement. They looked surprisingly young, or was it only that she was growing older? Their mode of dress would have brought stern disapproval in Shane's day. Many of the girls were clad in tight-fitting faded levis, and they wore blouses and shirts with an air of studied shabbiness, odd bits of jewelry strung on leather thongs. The boys dressed much the same, even to the jewelry, and she reflected that what with the long hair and the unisex clothing one could sometimes ascertain the sex only by a mustache or a shirtfront. Here and there a neat sweater and skirt or trimly cut head of hair looked almost out of place.

The house which had been her childhood home was a block off campus and she wandered there along the wide, tree-shaded street, looking at half-familiar homes, prim and well kept and touched but little by the years. The president's house, a large white imposing structure with two-story columns, stood at the end of a curving graveled driveway, guarded by wrought-iron gates.

Uncle Gregory's had been that white saltbox on the corner, set back from the street among sheltering maples. Shane got a jolt of surprise at the sight of childern's toys littering the yard, and a bright yellow Volkswagen in the driveway. She stared at it and laughed aloud. It bore a bumper sticker: *Support Your Local Fuzz.*

She ate her lunch in the student union. That, at least, had not changed; the food was as bad as she remembered it, and it was not difficult to understand why so many of the students seemed to be lunching on candy bars, potato chips, and Cokes.

She gave a sudden exclamation of pleasure. At a table beside a window, bent over coffee, sandwich, and a book, was a white-haired man with a thin sensitive face. She hurried to him.

"Doctor Rogers!" and as he got to his feet she held out her hand. "Do you remember me?"

"I do, indeed. Shane Parker—forgive me, Shane Manning now, isn't it? My dear, how are you? Please join me."

She complied, smiling at him. Frank Rogers had been her favorite of all the people at Tarant, her Latin instructor and, in his kindly, diffident way, her friend. He was a sweet-spirited man who had walked even then with a slight stoop, as if the burdens of the world weighed heavily upon him. He had often been at odds with Uncle Gregory as, indeed, who had not?

"It's been a long while, Shane."

"Yes. It's my first time back on the campus in more than ten years. I must say nothing seems to have changed too much."

"Well, change is coming—too slowly, I sometimes feel. We're still caught in the backwater. I think I should probably have left years ago, but I'm too old now to climb out of my comfortable rut until they push me out."

"Nonsense. I'm sure nothing would be the same without you."

"Well, things shouldn't remain the same, you know. There is some fresh water running into the pool, but I sometimes wonder if there aren't still too many of us old ones about, with out feet stuck fast in the ancient mud at the bottom. Tell me about yourself, and about Court. I have often wondered about you both."

"Court is well, and very busy. He has his own electronics firm and has made quite a success of it."

"I'm delighted to hear it. We were all shocked and saddened at the circumstances of his leaving Tarant, and the last time I spoke with him, I'm afraid he was very bitter."

"I know. It was a dreadful business, and Court never really got over it. I suppose he never will."

She hesitated, then met his glance candidly. "We're—having problems, just now; at any rate I am. It's why I'm here, to try to get some things sorted out in my own mind."

"I'm sorry. If there's any way I can help—"

"Thank you, no. I'm sure the trouble is mostly with me." She smiled faintly. "There just wasn't much in the way I was raised to gear me for the way the world really is. Court seems to have adjusted better than I—at least he seems to know what he wants and how to go about getting it."

"It's important, of course, knowing what one wants. Do you know, Shane?"

"No," she said, honestly, "not anymore. It's what I'm trying to find out. Maybe it's a pity I can't go back to school to learn."

"You were a fine student. The kind a teacher remembers. A bit timid and withdrawn, it's true—I remember I used to feel you had tremendous capabilities if someone could only draw you out."

"Well, thank you for that, although I'm afraid no one ever did. I really haven't done much with my life—nothing of any importance, certainly."

They were both silent for a space until Shane said, "It's delightful at the lake this time of year. I'd love it if you would drive up someday while I'm here. By the way, I've renewed acquaintance there with a priest, Father Francis Doheny. Do you know him?"

"Only slightly, through a nephew of his, a Doctor Kendall. He heads the psychology department here."

"Yes, I was going to ask you about him. I haven't met him, but his uncle mentioned him and I was curious. He sounds rather unusual for Tarant College."

"He is. It caused something of a stir when they took him on here. I must confess I was a bit on the fence about him at first. He's a clever chap, excellent writer—he's had any number of things published and they're quite good. As a person I like him well enough. I'm simply not clear on how well he fits into our pattern here. He has a certain intellectual arrogance that disturbs me, or perhaps I'm just not seeing very clearly across the generation gap. Certainly the students think highly of him. I've always felt that to teach the young wants a sort of humility, and I don't detect much of that in Doctor Kendall. He's what your uncle used to call a freethinker," a small smile tugged at the corners of his mouth, "which is probably no indictment in itself. But first the young have to be taught to think for themselves, not just to admire and emulate someone who can." He broke off. "I'm talking too much."

"Nothing of the sort. I did ask you."

"To be truthful, Doctor Kendall has been a bit

of a sore point with me. As I say, there was quite a to-do when the regents approved his appointment. There's still a great deal of opposition to him, among some of our older faculty members, who would like very much to see him taken out. I have defended him, sometimes without being quite certain it was the right thing to do. Still, you made a point when you mentioned Tarant's not having geared you for the world out there. Maybe that's the ability Kendall has and some of us simply don't care to own up to our lack of it."

They left the building presently and strolled together across the campus. They passed the chapel and Shane queried, "Are the students still required to attend here?"

"Not anymore. It was a long while in coming—Gregory Parker once made the remark that he'd die before he'd see them rescind the compulsory chapel rule, and I'm afraid that's precisely how it had to be." Then he seemed to remember, belatedly, that he was speaking to Gregory Parker's niece. "I'm sorry, my dear."

"Don't be. I used to sit through all those interminable services and vow that when I was old enough to choose, I would never go to church again. As a matter of fact, I seldom have." There seemed no point in adding that this was mainly because Court flatly refused to go, contending that the church was full of hypocrites and he did not choose to join their ranks.

Rogers said, equably, "I'm sorry to hear it. In any case, don't use what you knew of Tarant chapel as a benchmark. You must remember, Gregory always had a crop of young preachers coming on, and he simply provided them with a place to practice and a captive congregation to practice on. Your uncle was a good man, Shane. In his time, training young ministers was the chief function of Tarant, and it was what he knew best. I often suspected that in the later days he suspected the change that was coming and resisted it in the only way he knew. I don't think he could have found it within himself to face the truth, that a school like Tarant could not survive in this changing world."

"Poor Uncle Gregory."

"He was a good man," he said again, "a man deeply dedicated to what he believed. At the last, I think, he was a deeply troubled man."

"Troubled?"

"He was old and tired, and meeting increasing opposition at every turn. It isn't an easy thing for a man who has devoted himself, his life, to building something, to see younger, fresher people moving in, eager to tear it down and rebuild it to their own ideas. Even I could see that unless we encouraged our young seminary men to look at the realities of today's world, understand them, and prepare to cope with them at all levels, then the seminary—perhaps even the church itself—could not hope to survive. It's the curse too many of us are under, I daresay, not knowing when the time has come to step down and let the young have their turn at building. The world we knew is all but gone—and too many of us are frightened by the new one."

Shane was silent, turning something over in her mind. She had known only resentment toward Uncle Gregory for so long, to feel a stir of pity for him now was a strange thing.

When she said good-bye to her old friend, he clasped her hands. "Whatever it is that's troubling you, I hope you find your answers soon."

"Thank you. It's been wonderful, talking to you."

"Listening to me, you mean." His smile was rueful. "I got off at a tangent and I'm afraid I monopolized the conversation."

"Not at all. You've helped me understand my uncle a bit—but then you're the first person I've ever talked to who seemed to understand him."

"Then I'm glad. May I say something to you, Shane? Don't go to church, if you choose not to. I don't recall reading much about Jesus going to church very often, except to take issue with the way people there were behaving themselves. But don't rule God out, whatever you do. He may just turn out to be the only chance any of us has got." Suddenly his tired old face crinkled into a youthful, mischief-touched smile, and he patted her arm. "Keep the faith, baby."

It had been an interesting day and she arrived home in the evening pleasantly tired, glad to be back within the walls of her cottage. Idly she wondered why this house had such a pull for her, almost an enchantment—a much stronger attachment than anything she could ever feel for her handsome, ultraconvenient Regency home. If it was nostalgia, certainly it was for something intangible, not for the people whose memories it evoked.

My parents are too far gone into the past for me to think of them with anything but a faint unhappiness, and even if Doctor Rogers did manage to make me feel a bit sorry for Uncle Gregory, I'm certain I could never feel homesick for him.

I have often felt sorry for myself because there have been so few people who loved me. In all my life, how many people have I ever really, truly loved?

One. It was a sobering thought. *Only one. Only Court.*

Here in this cottage she felt cradled and safe,

although had she been asked, "Safe from what?" she could not have said.

When she slept that night, she dreamed that Court came walking up the flagstone path, across the terrace, and he stood outside, looking in at her.

"Come in," she said.

"I can't. You've locked the door."

"Then break it down."

He beat vainly against the door and she looked at his bleeding hands and began to weep.

"Don't you know why you can't come in, Court? Because I'm not your mother!"

On a crisp blue morning she delved through cupboards and boxes, looking for fishing gear. In a closet she found a rod, ancient but in fair condition. She assembled lines and leaders and flies and put them into a kit. Getting into pants and a bulky sweater, she carried her equipment down to the water's edge.

Her first cast went wildly into the trees above her and she stood looking in dismay at line hopelessly entangled among pine branches, dangling tauntingly out of her reach. An amused voice said from behind her, "That might be fine for birds, if you can throw straight enough, but I doubt you'll get many fish up there."

A tall man, wearing disreputable Levi's and an

old leather jacket, stood grinning at her. Well, laughing at her was what he was doing, actually. When he walked toward her and said, "Let me help with that," her rejoinder was coolly dignified.

"Thank you, but I can get it down myself." She hadn't any notion how and she certainly meant to wait for him to go away before she made any attempt.

"I wasn't thinking of getting it down. I'm afraid that isn't a very climbable tree. Best thing would be to cut the line and start over. It's a shame to cut your rig, but I'm afraid it can't be helped."

"It doesn't matter. It's old and not much good anyway." Then her sense of humor overcame her injured dignity and she began to laugh. "I should have known I wouldn't be any good at this. When I was a very little girl my father tried to teach me, but he wasn't very patient. He shouted at me, and I got upset and threw it anywhere except where it was supposed to go. I never tried it again."

"Well, as a teacher myself I'm opposed to shouting, but I'll be glad to show you whatever I can. By the way, I'm Jeff Kendall. You would be Shane Manning. My uncle told me about you."

"Yes, he spoke of you to me, too. I understand you're at Tarant. My uncle used to be dean of the seminary there."

"I've heard considerable about him. Bit of a holy terror, wasn't he?"

She laughed again and nodded, and thought, Well, I've heard about you, too. Are you really arrogant?

She fished with him that first day, and she caught fish under his expert tutelage, and that evening she went to a fish fry at the priest's cottage.

"I assure you," the younger man told her gravely, "none of the proprieties will be outraged, not with the good padre, my uncle, to chaperone us."

After dinner the three of them sat outside on the roofless deck which overhung the water's edge, watching the day die over the water and the moon lift, laying a white path across the calm surface. They talked of this and that, Jeff and his uncle falling now and then into the amiable wrangling which seemed to characterize their relationship. She thought the younger man an intriguing conversationalist and she liked listening to his deep lively voice. He had a quirky sense of humor and a deft way with an anecdote. Idly she mused, I'll wager he's popular with his students, especially the girls.

He walked her home and insisted on coming inside to light a fire for her against the September night chill. In the parlor he stood looking about him with undisguised pleasure.

"This is great! Authentic turn of the century."

"Isn't it? I've always adored the place."

"I don't wonder." His glance fell on an ivory chess set in a glass-topped case on the mantel. "That's a handsome thing."

"It was hand-carved for my father by an African native, years ago. My parents were there on some missionary chore or other."

"I've heard of them. It must have been interesting, having such peripatetic parents. Did you get to go with them on many of their junkets?"

Shane said, "They took me to Fort Worth, Texas, once," and an odd edge to her words warned him off. He ran his fingertips across the chess box.

"Do you play?"

"Rather badly."

"Good. I'm at my finest with a bad player. The next rainy afternoon, look for me to come knocking at your door. Meanwhile, will I see you in the morning? If you get to the lake before I do, try to keep your line out of the trees, right?"

In retrospect she would recognize that he had an almost instant physical attraction for her, but at first she acknowledged only that she liked him and felt at ease with him; and perhaps she did wonder, idly, what it would be like to have a man like Jeff Kendall make love to her.

She was usually inclined to be diffident with strangers, particularly of the academic variety, but their backgrounds and mutual acquaintances gave them something in common and made them a bit less than strangers from the beginning. She did not detect in him any of the arrogance of which Doctor Rogers had spoken. Confidence, that was more like it, a sureness of himself. She liked that in him.

It was with a quality of amazement that she began to realize Jeff was attracted to her, too. Her life had been so sheltered, so insular, that it had never occurred to her there might be anyone but Court, certainly not a man of Jeff Kendall's sort, who would find her desirable.

In her memory, those first days would run together, a pleasant blur, and she would be able to pick from them only fragmented moments, like bright islands.

"—It was incredible, the way it was with me, as if I were quite another person, not Shane Manning—" With a husband at home.

"When I saw you there at the lake that first morning I thought 'That woman has the unhappiest eyes I have ever seen.' Uncle Francis had said you were an attractive woman and when I met you, I told him I agreed. He reminded me that you are a married woman, and I said, 'It can't be a very happy marriage, can it, for her eyes to look like that?'"

"You'd have been unhappy, too, with your fishing line all tangled up in a tall pine tree and a stranger standing there laughing at you."

"Don't make a joke of it. When you laugh your face lights up, but when the laughter is gone your eyes look the way the lake does when a cloud passes over it. That first night I dreamed I heard someone crying. I knew it was you and I went looking for you, calling your name all along the shore, but I couldn't find you—"

She attempted, halfheartedly, to warn herself— he's probably an expert at the love game, he knows all the things to say to you to make you go all quivery inside—and she did not care. It was beautiful, and great fun, and she did not concern herself with the fact that it was undoubtedly insane. She was totally absorbed in building her bright islands to remember when it was over.

That funny little place in Tarant where he took her ... "You'll laugh at me, but this is the first time I ever had a drink with a man in a bar." There was a wooden plaque over the fireplace reading: *Tarant's Oldest and Best. Est. 1943.* "I was born in 1948 and I lived in this town for the first eighteen years of my life and never knew this place was here. Of course, I didn't know anything about drinking, either. I'm sure the strongest thing in Uncle Gregory's house was sherry, and that was only for the grownups on state occasions. I remember hearing people tell about how for years only one liquor license was available in this area—it had something to do with population density—and the board of regents bought it up and held it for years so no one could sell hard liquor near the campus."

There were couples at other tables, and perhaps a half dozen patrons at the bar. Their talk was quiet, but now and then a little ripple of laughter washed through the dimly lighted room. From a jukebox, music played softly and occasionally a couple arose and danced on the postage-stamp floor.

"Would you care for another drink before dinner?"

"Thank you, no. I've had my two. I never have more than that, even at home." She flushed with the realization that she had said it almost primly, as if to remind them both who and what she was—never more than two, at home with her husband.

Jeff appeared not to notice. "Incidentally, be it known that I don't consider you a bar type, but this is a quiet place and they have the best steaks in town. Later in the evening they have a folk singer I think you may enjoy."

"It's really very nice. I am enjoying it." She

was watching a dancing couple and thinking a trifle wistfully that Court had always disliked dancing. He was quite adequate at it, but he said it made him feel silly.

Jeff was watching her. He touched her hand and said, "You should see your eyes. You look like a kitten watching other cats play, not quite sure whether you want to join them or run away. Come on, I want to dance with you."

They talked endlessly, of all the cabbage-and-king and sealing-wax things that helped them get to know each other. Some of Jeff's viewpoints, she admitted privately, made her a trifle defensive because they were so clearly at odds with the attitudes she had held all her life. His position on marriage rankled a trifle.

"We're a multilevel social structure now and one set of mores for the whole push just won't cut it. I'm not against marriage. It's great for two people so much in love that they have a very real, basic need to belong to each other in just that way—and I'm sure it's still a must for those who want families. But it should be an individual option, not an antiquated tribal custom which retains the full force and effect of law."

She was moved to protest. "Surely you don't teach your students that!"

"Not directly." Her protest seemed to amuse

him. "In fact, it may be the students who have taught it to me."

She put down her impulse to speak out firmly in defense of marriage. It was only an automatic impulse—there was a faint cynicism in the thought. She and Court would not be raising a family, and they had not felt that urgent need to be together in a long while now, so what had she to defend?

She reflected that perhaps Jeff's attitudes toward the young were more broadly permissive than Doctor Rogers could wish them to be, but he recognized their problems with honesty and concern. The world they were growing up into, he said, was no Sunday-school picnic and insofar as was humanly possible they needed to be prepared for it. Otherwise, one was only teaching them to stick their heads in the sand and hope for the best.

He had an awakening effect on her mind. She had evaluated her life only in terms of her marriage, with its increasing frustrations and disappointments, for so long, that she had been no more than vaguely aware of the things outside the narrow boundaries of her own world. Jeff made her feel as if for a very long while she had been moving along a gloomy corridor, but now stood in an open doorway, seeing only dimly after the darkness, aware of the activity outside even if she were as yet unable to enter into it.

She liked being with Jeff. She knew what might happen between them, and with total self-honesty she accepted the truth. She wanted it to happen.

With her upbringing, it followed that lurking in the back of her consciousness was the awareness that an affair with Jeff must bring its consequences, but she told herself firmly that she did not care—and she declined to inquire of herself, when she was moved repeatedly to reaffirm the declaration, whether she was protesting too much.

Father Francis must have been uneasily forewarned by the way the two of them spent so much time together; it was he who unwittingly precipitated the inevitable. He was sitting with Shane on the deck of his cottage. They were watching Jeff, silhouetted against the red evening sky, beaching the boat from which he and Shane had been fishing all day. That afternoon he had kissed her, for the first time, a long searching caress in which all the important questions were asked, and answered. Now, Shane acknowledged with a shiver of anticipation, she was committed.

She said, "He is a marvelous person. You must be very proud of him."

"He is a gifted person." Father Francis sent white puffs of pipe smoke into the quiet air and squinted thoughtfully at them. "A strange man, in ways. For all that he is treating himself to a sort of sabbatical just now, I've known few who could drive themselves the way Jeffrey can, when he chooses. His work, his writing, those are more important to him than anything in the world. Just now he must teach in order to live, but I sometimes think it's not good, either for him or his students." His slight smile leavened the indictment. "It's just as well that he will probably never marry. One would be obliged to pity the woman who must try to cope with him. He believes happiness comes only with total freedom, and too often this puts him at war with the conventions."

He paused, but she was silent, thinking, You're warning me, of course.

"I'm afraid Jeffrey is the product of a generation which has attempted to persuade itself, with more success than I like to see, that the only real wrong is in hurting others. It follows, therefore, that a private sin which hurts no one else is no sin at all. That's only a humanist creed and a dangerous one, to my way of thinking. It has been my experience in this life that if we don't control the sin, we have no control over the consequences, to ourselves or others. We toss the pebble, the ripples spread— and it's not in our power to keep other lives from being touched, perhaps harmed." Then he gave her an apologetic smile. "Forgive me, my dear. I am so accustomed to quarreling with Jeffrey's views that I do it even when he is *in absentia*."

Shane arose and said, somewhat curtly, "I think I'll walk on back. I'm tired, and I've a case of sunburn I should attend to. Will you say good night to Jeff for me?"

She plodded grimly homeward, her resentment against the priest heightened by her own awareness that there was substance in what had been patently a warning, and never mind the small apology.

If her abrupt departure had been a bit on the childish side, it had not been designed to bring Jeff storming to her cottage, to demand, "Why did you run away like that? Look here, has Uncle Francis been saying anything to upset you?"

"Not really," she denied, but her tone was cross. She was bundled into an old woolly robe, her feet bare, and she felt weary and disheveled. She added, irritably, "I simply wanted to get a shower—and why are you staring at me like that?"

"I was wondering," Jeff said, gravely, "if you would let me come and help you with your shower." He made a little movement toward her and she walked into his arms. With his mouth against hers, he asked, "You know that this afternoon was only the prelude?"

"Yes," said Shane. "I know."

She would wonder, in a time yet to come, at the calm deliberation with which she surrendered herself to a sexual affair with Jeff. One might have thought that the very fact of the priest's tacit disapproval of their friendship, his ever-presence, would have discouraged her, since all her life had been lived subject to and apprehensive of the approval of others. Only once before, when she eloped with Court, had she had the courage to say, "This is what I want to do and I am going to do it."

Perhaps to be able to rebel only when one had a firm accomplice was no rebellion at all. What was needed, clearly, was more courage of her own before she could hope to emerge from her indecision and stand forth as a person, with confidence in her own ability to decide the course of her life.

She did not permit her mind to dwell on what might be the emotional aftermath of a brief affair with Jeff. She loved him in a different way than she loved Court.

I didn't know anything about loving, and Court didn't know how to teach me. I think his love for me is a need to possess, and that what I feel for Jeff is something Court has never known, either.

She was determined not to let her feeling for Jeff tumble her into any tender trap. She merely accepted it, in full knowledge that the affair would be of brief duration and inevitable ending. When it was over there would be times when she would miss him, need him; when she would be homesick for those golden lost days and nights at Shadow Lake with him. They would pass, and she would be a more complete woman because of her memories.

Now she was going home, a different Shane, and only she would have changed, she was certain of that. Court would be the same, and perhaps things would not work out between them.

It's what I want, for things to be right between Court and me, but I will face that when the time comes, on my own, making my own decisions.

She contemplated these things gravely in her final hours at the lake, and she gained an odd strength in the knowledge that it was she who was ending the affair. Still, there were bad moments when she wanted to say to Jeff, "Every time I think of leaving you I die a little."

That would spoil everything. He would be disappointed in her, denying her gently, and she would be humiliated. No regrets, no guilt, and no future—she would treasure what she had known with him, the loving, the laughter, his kindness that was more truly understanding than that of many whose fear of the moral conventions made them furtive about their own transgressions.

I will remember Jeff with love, and I will get over loving him.

And Court?

Perhaps she could love Court in a way that had nothing to do with Jeff, and if a part of what she offered him was counterfeit, he need never know. She would atone to him for a wrong he would never know had been done him, and she would no longer hold to his account the wrongs he had done her.

9.

Regency Road was a loose circle of homes facing upon a common green with a golf course, a lake, tennis courts, and swimming pools. There was a sprawling handsome clubhouse, membership in which was the automatic right of Regency owners, subject to bylaws drawn up by the owners' association and administered by a select committee. The road itself was a pivotal point for the large community of affluent "suburban estates" surrounding it—a walled community with a security gatehouse and patrolling guard.

By tacit acknowledgment Regency aristocracy lived on the road. The homes there were the most expensive; they fronted the lake, which was large enough for small boating, waterskiing, and angling for the trout planted there periodically by the fish-and-game people. Each had its private dock and boathouse.

Regency was one of the subdivisions which had sprung up with an incredible swiftness in suburban areas in the past two decades. It had been fully completed for only about five years. Its inhabitants were cordial for the most part, united in a common prideful awareness, but they were still too new to each other to have formed deep and lasting friendships. A hundred-thousand-dollar neighborhood, Court called it, meaning it was the average cost of a Regency "estate" and not, Shane was wryly aware, that all who lived there could afford it. *From* $100,000, that was how the real-estate brochures said it. The houses on the road proper came in considerably above the *from*.

One suspected that for some Regency owners it was a tight squeeze, and that it might be those who lived in a sort of competitiveness with the others, keeping up with everyone and struggling to make it appear no struggle at all.

The Mannings could afford it, a fact of which Court was very proud. He was prone to poke fun at Regency's "social director," who tried valiantly to put together a group-oriented social agency for the community; nevertheless he wanted the Manning name known in Regency. For him, to be able to attain to this standard of living seemed a part of some dream come true.

It had been a bit less than that for Shane. She had not wanted to leave the house on Peach Street, in the small semirural community where they had lived before Manning Enterprises began making what Court called "real money," before he had decided Peach Street and its neighborhood were no longer right.

He had been infinitely annoyed when Shane resisted the idea. "I'm damned if I understand you. I'd think you'd be glad to get out of this place."

"What's wrong with it?"

"What's right with it?" They were sitting on the porch and his glance traveled critically over what they could see of the street. Even if she were not in a like frame of mind, she could summon enough imagination to see it through his eyes—the eyes of a vigorous, ambitious young man. It was remarkable what Court had already accomplished before he was well into his thirties—a solid, steadily growing bank account; a solid, steadily growing business; solid credit. He had cause to be proud.

Peach Street houses were old, designed to be functionally comfortable rather than handsome. They were close together, and many of the yards were strewn with children's toys. The noisy neighborhood kids annoyed Court.

He had no such problem at Regency. It was an adult community for the most part, and the few families with youngsters were relegated to a separate area, the "young family" section—a kind of plush ghetto, Shane thought with some irony, for the very young. Their own Regency house would remain pristine, of course, unsullied by young hands.

Whenever Shane thought of that now it was with a vague passive resentment almost too old and too comfortable to arouse the heat of an old anger.

She had outgrown, only slowly, the period during which she had been unable to keep a companionable pace with Court in his absorbed struggle to the "top of the pile." What was the top to him? she had wondered bleakly. By what standards did he judge where his own pinnacle lay? By his choice, his blood kin were no part of his life; he had not chosen to have sons and daughters of his own. What satisfaction could there be in standing alone on his own private peak, with family and even love lost in a forgotten valley he had left behind him?

For Shane, Peach Street was the village at the foot of the mountain. It was the world to which Court had brought her as a bride; her few friends were there; if she had any roots at all, they were there.

She had been helplessly aware that Court was keenly disappointed by her initial reaction to Regency. "You'll like it fine when we've been there for a while and you get acquainted." When she had been slow to prove him right in that, he complained irritably, "I don't know what your problem is. Most women would jump at the chance to get a home like this while they're still young enough to enjoy it. You aren't the easiest person in the world to get to know, not with that standoffishness of yours. It wouldn't hurt you to put yourself out a little, instead of waiting for people to come to you."

It was obvious what her problem was, of course. She was a product of the smallest of all possible worlds. In her lifetime she had known only Tarant, where she had been born and raised, and Peach Street. She was not gregarious by nature, even if she had overcome to an extent the painful timidity which had plagued her as a child. Transition was an ordeal for her, but after a time, to please Court, she had ventured at least into the edge of the mainstream of Regency life. Apparently she had more to offer than she had thought, because she had been readily accepted.

Court was pleased. "You know something? I was actually beginning to wonder if I'd done wrong, taking you away from Peach Street. You were behaving like a homesick kid."

It was a homesickness—that she acknowledged—but unlike Court she could not equate it simply with a longing for familiar faces or places.

The truth is, I think I am homesick for some place I have never been and for someone I have never known.

Her world had been dominated almost completely by males. On Peach Street she had friendly female acquaintances whose company she enjoyed mildly, although she was not really close to any of them. Even their small daily lives seemed filled with matters with which she was unfamiliar, and she could not identify with them.

On Regency Road, with time, and in a manner of speaking, Dee Andreas had come to be the first close woman friend she had ever had.

The Andreas home was next to the Mannings. Art Andreas, a dark taciturn man, owned a restaurant and bar in one of the older sections of the city, and a chain of hamburger drive-ins scattered throughout the metropolitan area. His background did not fit too smoothly with the image some Regency people liked to maintain, but he had sufficient capital at his command to buy or sell any of them, and financial status was the prime concern of the Regency promoters. They left the social amenities and problems to the residents.

Art's wife, Dee, was a handsome blonde. She had a calm, assured awareness of her sex which amused Shane and outraged some of the other Regency wives. They traded gossip that she had been a chip girl in a Las Vegas casino and that Art was her third—or was it her fourth?— husband. Some of them kept a sharp eye on their own husbands when Dee was around.

To Shane, she confided the truth, that she had been a hostess in Art's cocktail lounge. "That's a cut above hasher, and you get to wear slinky evening things instead of a uniform. The pay's not so hot, but the tips are good if you know your stuff."

Art was her second husband. Her first had been a good-looking truck driver, of whom she spoke with distaste. "He was sexy as hell, and not much else to go with it. He screwed around with every dame that waved it at him. We had a pretty sad marriage and it blew up in a couple of years.

Art is my second and last. He's good to me, and he doesn't screw around. He likes a woman with flash, so I play up to it. Blond isn't my color and I've spent so much of my life on my feet that if I had my way I'd never wear another pair of heels—but this is the way he likes me, and this is the way he'll get me. Don't spread it around, because I get my jollies out of worrying those broads over at the club, but I love the guy."

She was so merry, her laughter so infectious, that Court liked her, too, albeit grudgingly. Privately, Shane knew, he considered her common and vulgar. She chain-smoked, and at the club it was said she could hold her liquor as well as any man, and more of it than most. She made no real play for any of the men but she was fun loving and uninhibited, and when she had a glow on, her talk was apt to be spiced with four-letter words.

Though she was a thorn in Regency flesh sometimes, she was genuinely kind and honest, and Shane was fond of her. It was not an intimacy, they were too different, and for all their friendliness each had a boundary beyond which the other did not intrude. Their friendship was a relaxed and easy thing.

The taxi drew up before the Manning house. Shane glanced at its familiar outlines with eyes which did not really see it. It was a smart house set in a row of smart houses, all with impeccably landscaped and manicured grounds, all with that curious alikeness—handsome expressionless faces gazing aloofly at passersby.

One familiar with such houses could guess that the front door opened into a handsome foyer, beyond which lay the two-story, beamed-ceiling living room, with an imposing brick-fireplace wall, and an open stairway ascending to a balcony off which the guest rooms opened. There would be a great picture window overlooking a flagstone terrace, with a private pool, umbrella tables, a barbecue pit, many glossy vines and plants, those indispensable appurtenances to gracious outdoor living, all protected from the outside world by handsome redwood louvered fencing.

The driver carried Shane's bags to the door and set them inside for her. She paid him and he went away. She walked into the house, feeling its cool impersonal quiet settle about her. The place was immaculate, a tribute both to Court's orderliness and the twice-weekly ministrations of a cleaning woman.

She left her luggage in the foyer and went into the kitchen. Although it was past the lunch hour she was not hungry. She nibbled at a piece of celery from the crisper, made herself a cup of coffee, and carried it to the food bar, to drink it in solitary splendor.

The kitchen door bell gave its soft three-note chime. Shane slid off the stool and went to answer. Dee Andreas stood there, her hair rumpled and brassy in the sunlight, a broad smile on her face.

"Greetings. I saw your cab drive up, so I thought I'd just scoot in and say hello, welcome home, and all that jive."

"I'm having coffee. Come in and I'll share."

Dee settled herself at the bar, and Shane brought her a steaming cup. "What's new?"

"Not a whole lot. You want to hear some juicy gossip?"

Shane laughed and said, "Go."

"Well, Warren and Dorothy Trowbridge got stoned out of their skulls at the dinner dance Saturday night and threw a brawl right in the middle of the dance floor. Seems Warren sat out a couple in a dark corner with someone else's wife, and Dorothy threatened to pin his ears back. She popped him a couple of good ones before he managed to get her off the dance floor. There's some talk afloat about asking the Trowbridges to resign from the club. Art says forget it, the club just isn't that exclusive and the committee doesn't pack that much clout. Membership goes with the deed to the property, and it doesn't restrict any member from slapping her husband around. You can bet the Trowbridges are in for a royal snubbing, though."

"I suppose." That ought to solve Milly Eastman's problem about hanging Dorothy at the art exhibit this year. "Was Court there?"

"Through part of it, but when Warren and Dorothy began really mixing it up, I think he left."

"Probably. He hates a scene, and he particularly dislikes for Regency people to behave badly. He likes to think of us as—oh, rather select."

Dee hooted. "Select, my eye! If the Trowbridges hadn't happened to come into a wad of money when the new transcoast freeway sliced up their commercial property, they'd still be living on the east side and getting loaded in a beer joint on Saturday night." Then she slid from her stool. "I've got to get back to my own kitchen. I'm trying out a new recipe for curry, but it will probably come out tasting like the same old Spanish rice. Once in a while when you were away, I brought over stuff for Court to eat. I wouldn't have the nerve to ask him if he ate it or threw it out—he'll probably be relieved to get his feet back under your table again. Hey, it's good to have you home. You really look great. I wish some doc would tell me I had to take a nice long rest—fat chance. I don't have enough to do to get me tired as it is." She tossed a hand in blithe salute and went out, her round hips

209

swinging perkily. Shane looked after her bemusedly.

She knows exactly who and what she is, and she's happy with it. That's how I want to be.

She went into the master bedroom she shared with Court, to unpack a suitcase and begin to put things away, fingers lingering only briefly over the sleek sea-green sheath she had worn the night she went to dinner with Jeff in that little Tarant bar.

When she had completed her unpacking, she showered, and came back into the bedroom wrapped in a towel. Catching sight of herself in the full-length mirror of her open closet door she paused, letting the towel slide to the floor, gravely regarding what she saw, a small delicately made woman with smooth firm skin, good breasts, flat stomach. Her hair was fair and shone with good care. Her face was—well, a face. Good eyes, clear and wide spaced, a good enough nose, well-shaped mouth over good teeth.

A nice face, Jeff had said, as nice to look at in the morning as over a candle-lit dinner table. *"And there aren't many women who can make that claim, I'd imagine. It's why the cosmetic people are such fat cats."*

Was it really only this morning, only a few hours ago, that she had taken her leave of him? She had the weird sense that when she walked into this house, these familiar rooms had wrapped themselves tightly around her, and Jeff had receded swiftly into distance, a hazy *long time ago.*

She walked slowly toward the mirror and touched the reflected face with tentative fingertips, the way Jeff had often touched it. The glass was coldly smooth and impersonal beneath her touch. Suddenly she shivered as with a chill and stooped to retrieve the towel, covering her nakedness with it.

Court telephoned, wanting to make certain she had gotten home all right. He was sorry not to be able to get away to meet her plane, but he had this buyer in from Seattle, and had to finish with him. He'd see her at dinner time.

She was in the kitchen preparing a salad when she heard the wheels of his car crunch on the graveled driveway.

He was clearly glad to see her. He kissed her twice and patted her bottom and noted that the house had been lonely without her. She was looking great, and was she feeling better?

Oh, yes, much better. She was really feeling quite fit.

Had she had a nice time?

Yes, a lovely time.

"See anybody we used to know?"

"A few, although 'most everyone we might have known is gone. I did spend some time at the college one day, and I had a nice visit with Doctor Rogers. He asked about you." She paused, but when he made no comment she went on,

"The only lake cottage near me that was occupied was the old Miller place, across the cove. A priest has it now, a Father Francis Doheny. He knew my family, and I remembered him vaguely. I met a nephew of his, a Doctor Jeffrey Kendall. He teaches at Tarant."

There, I have said his name and nothing in the way I said it made Court look at me strangely, and I felt no guilt.

"He heads the psychology department at the college—he's a writer, too. I saw quite a lot of them. They taught me how to fish."

Court grinned. "Priests and college professors— it sounds like you were traveling in the egghead league. It's nice you had someone to visit with. I'd think it could be pretty deadly up there this time of year. To tell you the truth, I didn't think you'd stick it as long as you did."

That seemed to exhaust his interest in her trip. After dinner he settled himself in his chair and unfolded his newspaper. He suspended it in midair to say, "Oh, by the way, your women's club is sponsoring some sort of concert over at the center tonight—chamber music, whatever the hell that is. Would you like to go?"

She hid her surprise. "I don't think so, but thank you, anyway," and as he leaned back in his chair with an almost audible sigh of relief she thought, It was sweet of him to offer, especially since he loathes that kind of music.

For a moment she studied him dispassionately. Court was really a good-looking man, lean and trim, his hair dark and glossy. *A more handsome man than Jeff Kendall, actually.*

After a time she went into the bedroom and returned with a slim volume. Court glanced up.

"New book?"

"Jeff Kendall gave it to me." She was aware that she was deliberately bringing Jeff's name up so Court would be casually aware of him, and no inadvertent reference to him by Shane would cause her self-consciousness. "He wrote it. It's a comparative study of ancient and modern methods of dealing with mental disorders."

He made a little sound of derision. "Sounds about as exciting as last year's seed catalogue."

She rejoined lightly, "Well, since he was kind enough to give it to me, I suppose the least I can do is try and read it, although I probably won't understand a word of what he's talking about." She made a mental apology to Jeff for passing off his award-winning work so lightly.

After a time Court muttered, "Good God!" and Shane glanced up inquiringly.

"You remember Brad Ellers, on Peach Street? He's been arrested for murder. He shot his wife."

"Brad killed Alida? Oh, Court, how horrible!"

"Seems he was away on a hunting trip and came home unexpectedly. There was Alida with some man, and he just opened up on them. Shot at the guy, too, but only wounded him. How about that? As far as anyone knows, two people are happily married and then *blam!* Right out of the blue."

Shane considered it, frowning. "Well, I suppose it's obvious they weren't all that happily married, or why would Alida have done such a thing?"

"A woman like that, you never can tell. They go along for years and you think they're just like anyone else, and then with no warning at all—"

A woman like that. There you had it, hadn't you? From a husband's eye view, all done up in a neat parcel.

Maybe Alida did try to warn Brad in some way of her own, but if I know Brad he wasn't listening. He never listened to her.

"Well, I'm sorry for him, of course, although I never liked him much. He was always the center of everything, always rambling on and on, usually about himself, making everyone else listen, and poor Alida just sitting there and never saying

214

anything. She wasn't stupid, but I don't think I ever heard her venture an opinion of her own. Brad was always putting her down. You never liked him much either, I seem to recall."

"Actually, the guy was pretty much of a jerk, but that doesn't mean he should be fair game for any guy who wanted to go to bed with his wife, does it?"

"Of course not, but killing her—is that what you'd advocate?"

"Sure." He laughed a little. "Open season, especially if you find them in bed together."

She watched him. "I don't think you believe that at all. Suppose," she was aghast at her own daring; it was crazy, like walking deliberately, perilously close to the edge of a precipice, "that you were in Brad's place?"

What in the name of God is the matter with you? Do you *want* him to know?

It was insane, a part of her mind splitting away like that. Court stopped laughing and she held her breath with a sudden sensation very like fear.

"Don't talk rot, Shane. You could no more do something like that than I could. That wasn't very funny."

She said, gently, "No, I guess it wasn't."

It was a little past eleven when he switched off the television. He got to his feet, yawned, stretched, and crossed the room to stand beside

Shane and touch her shoulder with tentative fingers.

"You about ready to come to bed?"

"Yes." She looked down at her book, closed it. Then she smiled up at Court. "Yes, I'm ready."

On Saturday night they went to the dinner dance at the club. It was a concession Court made dutifully to Regency amenities. He did not care for the food at the club, but they would dine. They would not dance.

She wore the green sheath, feeling a kind of perversity as she slid into it, hearing Jeff's voice, *Come on, I want to dance with you.*

What was that song? *I saw a man, he danced with his wife—*

Not this man. Not this wife.

When she came into the living room, Court observed, "You look nice. New dress?"

"I bought it in Tarant."

"Looks good on you."

She was touched. Court seldom noticed what she wore. They were, she thought with some amusement, being very nice to each other—or perhaps Court was only responding to something a bit nicer in her.

He was studying her. "You're different. There's some color and life about you."

"Thank you." *A man looked at me and really*

saw me, and he wanted me. He made me feel lovely and desirable. Have you any idea what that can mean?

"You are better, aren't you?"

"Of course. I've told you I am."

"Well, I'm glad now we took David Price's advice. To tell you the truth, I had my doubts. It didn't seem to me you were in any condition to go knocking off on your own—and I guess I didn't like the idea of rattling around in this big house without you. It wasn't my idea of the way to get things straightened out, even if we did seem to be fighting a lot of the time. Once I almost came up there after you, but then I thought, no, give it a chance. If she can stand it up there alone, I can stand it here alone."

She said in a small shaken voice, "Oh, Court," and put her arms around him. "You mustn't worry about me anymore."

For an instant his hand strayed down, seeking the curve of her hip. "If we're going to the club it'd better be now, otherwise I'm not going to be in any shape—"

The unaccustomed ribaldry from him surprised her, and she was vaguely pleased to feel a faint stir of desire. She whirled away from him, laughing. "Behave yourself. You invited me to dinner, and I got all turned out for you, so come along." She kissed him lightly. "Any other ideas you have we can take up later."

He grinned at her, abashed, but she sensed that he was pleased, with her and with himself.

The club was nearby and they walked over. After dinner they strolled homeward, hand in hand through the California-mild autumn evening, by the faint light of a rising moon.

"This is almost like being back on campus, remember?"

"Of course, I remember. I loved being with you. It was the most important thing in my life."

"Every time I'd take you home I'd think, 'This will be the night old Gregory the Dragon comes roaring out of his lair and tells me to stay the hell away from her.'"

"Well, he did complain to me, but I'm sure he understood I was going to go on seeing you, no matter how he felt about it."

His hand tightened its grasp on hers. "While you were away, I did a lot of thinking. For a long time it had seemed to me as if we might have reached the end of the road. It wasn't what I wanted, but nothing seemed to be going right."

"I know."

"Having that operation, going about everything the way I did—that was stupid. I've tried to think of some way to make it up to you."

"That's behind us. I've done a lot of thinking, too. The state of mind and emotion I had let myself drift into—I can understand it better now. I was just existing, and that's not good. There are so many things, exciting things, going on in the world—I'm not going to make the same mistakes again. I want to get *involved.*"

"Well, there's your art association and everything. You were pretty involved in that."

"Oh, darling, that's not the sort of thing I mean. It's only a hobby, without any real substance or meaning. I'm thinking of something like volunteer work in a hospital. Maybe I'd even like to go back to school and get my degree, equip myself to do something more meaningful." It was a trite phrase, but at the moment she could not think of a better one; and clearly now was the time, if ever, to let Court know what was in her mind.

"What for?" He was genuinely puzzled. "I don't know what you need money for that I can't provide."

"It has nothing to do with money, only with being useful! It's why I was thinking of volunteer work. Just now I'd count myself fortunate to have someone accept my services free of charge!"

Court released her hand and they walked for a distance in silence.

"Honey, I wish I could understand what you're driving at, but I don't. You've got a beautiful home, with more than enough in it to keep you as busy as you want to be. You've hobbies you enjoy, new friends—what more do you want?"

"A lot more." She drew a deep breath and chose her words with care. "I want something that has some real significance for *me*—why should you find that so difficult to understand? Obviously I can't be a great painter or violinist, or go into politics, or join the Peace Corps—but there has to be something I can do. Maybe it's that I need something I can feel about the way you feel about Manning Enterprises."

"It's not the same thing. Manning Enterprises is my work, and I do it as much for you as for myself, maybe more."

"Still, it is something you put a lot of yourself into. You derive pride from it, and a sense of achievement."

"And you can't do the same with your home, and being my wife."

"I'm sorry—no, I can't. If we'd had children—" Oh, God, she hadn't meant to say that, but it was out and he pounced on it.

"I thought you said that was in the past! You aren't going to let it alone, are you?"

"I only meant that even with all the wonderful things you do for me, there is something lacking. Can't you see that it is a part of what was wrong with me? I need to be doing something with my own life—at least to find out what I'm capable of doing. Maybe nothing, but I need to know. I hoped you would understand, and want to help."

"I am trying to understand and I do want to help. Everything I do is for you, for us, and if that isn't enough—"

She interposed wearily, "Please don't make it sound as if I'm accusing you of letting me down. You've done wonderfully well and I'm proud of that. The point is, I'd like to be able to be proud of myself for a change." I can't compromise with honesty now. If I withhold part of the truth this thing will only become more involved and in the end both of us will be losers! "Court, please don't lock me up in the frame of—of *housewife*, and take everything I say as a criticism of you as a husband. Just for a little bit, listen to me as another *person*."

"I don't know, Shane." He sounded tired and discouraged. "When you came home I thought you were feeling a lot better, and things could get back to being the way they used to be."

"I don't want them to be the way they used to be. That is exactly what I do not want!" Her voice rose sharply and Court stopped walking, to peer at her through the half-gloom.

"I don't know what's gotten into you, Shane. I'm not going to try to stop you from doing whatever you damned well want to do, but don't expect me to understand it, because I don't! Most women would be satisfied with half what you've got. My mother never had much of anything at all, but she never thought she had to go out and take some kind of job—"

"I am not your mother!" Even her surprise at his mentioning Adele for the first time in years did not abate the anger which jolted her. "The things I need from you have nothing to do with the sort of thing you did for her, and you've substituted me for her long enough!"

"Just what the hell," Court's voice went tight with fury, "is that supposed to mean?"

"It's the simple truth!" She was beyond caring now. "The domination, the overprotectiveness, expecting me to complete the dependence on you that she rejected—"

"If you think I'm going to listen to this—"

"Oh, face it, Court! I've had to." And when he turned away from her, going up the flagstone walk toward the house, she hurried after him. "Court—"

He did not pause. "I don't think you'd better say any more, Shane. I don't want to talk about it any more tonight."

"We will talk about it! That's always been an easy out for you, refusing to talk about something you don't care to face. It is a great part of what's been wrong between us all along, whether you care to acknowledge it or not! We've never really talked out the important things, not even the ones that were wrecking our marriage. If what I said about Adele offended you, I'm sorrier than I can say, but it is something I've had to live with all these years."

He halted, key in hand. "I'm going in to bed. Maybe you'll see things differently in the morning."

He disappeared into the house. For a moment Shane stood where she was; then her lips set grimly and she followed him inside.

"Don't walk away from me, Court—not this time. I'm going to say what's on my mind and you're going to listen! When I went up to Shadow Lake, I had pretty well made up my mind that I wasn't coming back. I know you thought I needed psychiatric treatment—David Price considered the possibility, only he said he had an idea I already knew what was causing my trouble, and he was right!"

Court switched on the lamp beside his chair and sat down heavily, looking at Shane with an air of angry resignation. "Go ahead," he said, tonelessly. "Get it all out, all the crazy ideas that are bothering you."

Shane shook her head. "Oh, no, not crazy. There was a while when I thought maybe I actually was losing my mind—but I was wrong. Would it surprise you if I say I think David knew perfectly well that a lot of my trouble was you?"

"So we're back to that. It's all my fault."

"I didn't say that, and I don't say you knew what you were doing to me; I'm sure you didn't. But we won't blame it all on me any longer, either. Did it ever occur to you that you might have been sicker than I was, and for longer?"

His face went slack with astonishment. "You are crazy."

"Oh, no, I'm really quite sane; I know that now. Just as I know I'm making you very angry, and I'm sorry about that, but if there is anything at all left for us together, we're not going to drag it to a dreary death! If I can't break through to you and make you understand, then I will go away, and this time I won't be back."

He exhaled angrily. "Don't threaten me, Shane."

"It's no empty threat. I'm only saying what I may have to do. You have lived for years with hatred for Waverly; you've fed on it, and to what end? You haven't punished him, only yourself, and me. What your mother did was tragic, it was horrible, and that's just it, the whole awful truth, *she did it herself!*" And at a furious gesture from him she said, sturdily, "No, I'm going to finish. Other people have gone through what she did, and worse, and survived. She chose not to try.

From the day it happened, you changed, and it wasn't a good change. It has affected our marriage—you've put me in her place so much, that I actually think sometimes when you made love to me you thought about her, and the things your father had done, and you were ashamed, as if you were doing something rotten!"

He looked stonily at her. "Are you through?"

Her shoulders sagged tiredly. "Yes, I guess I am."

"Then good night." He arose and walked out of the room and she heard him going through the hallway to their bedroom.

She switched off the lamp and lay on a divan, staring into the darkness, the rebellious unhappiness in her an actual physical pain.

I really wanted to come home; I wanted to believe that things might work out for Court and me, but it isn't going to be any good. I wish I had stayed with Jeff, for however long it might have lasted, and then gone about the business of living my own life.

She was still there in the morning, sleeping fitfully, fully clothed, when she heard Court get up and go into the kitchen. After a time the aroma of coffee came faintly to her, but she did not stir. She heard a shower running, heard Court moving about in the bedroom; then he went out of the house and his car left the driveway. It was the first time in ten years he had left the house to go to work without kissing her good-bye.

In the next few days, at breakfast and in all the intervals when they were together briefly, they said only the politely inconsequential things people must say when they live under the same roof. The estrangement which might have been avoided, Shane told herself bitterly, by a genuine give and take, a little understanding, was widening into a dark gulf no longer to be crossed by either of them.

10.

She had been at home for a week when she called Jeff, putting aside her agonized indecision. She had, after all, promised him she would call, to let him know how things were going for her.

Well, she could hardly tell him they were going the way she might have expected, had she not been carried away by her own blindingly new feeling of self-worth and assurance. She and Court were living in a kind of armed truce, courteous, uncommunicating. Shane had returned to her own bed in the room they shared, but he had not touched her since their quarrel and she was grateful for that.

Soon she must decide what she meant to do, and how to go about it, but for the present she was too dispirited to make the attempt. That this was a clear sign of her reverting to the old apathy, she knew, but she did not seem able to pull herself out. To reach Jeff again, if only for a few moments, across hundreds of miles of telephone line—yes, she wanted that.

If she had learned anything at all from Jeff, it was that one must be willing to take calculated risks, to be sure how much she was willing to give up to get to where she wanted to be.

I have felt guilty because I thought I owed something to Court, but there is a dividing line between what a woman owes her husband and what she owes herself. I have already used up too much of my life for nothing. If the rest isn't what I want it to be, then I'll have no one to blame but myself.

She placed the call in the morning, shortly after Court had left for his office.

If he sees the call on the telephone bill I'll

have to lie to him; I'll say I couldn't remember whether I asked Sam to winterize the cottage and I wanted Jeff or his uncle to stop by and speak to him.

If he asks why I didn't call Sam directly I'll say it was because I didn't know his last name, and at least that is the truth. If he ever told me, I have forgotten.

She had never lied to Court and she would be sorry for the necessity, but unless something changed now, and quickly, she would soon not be talking to Court about anything, ever again.

Jeff was not in his office, but a female voice said he had left word that he would be in at noon.

"Then would you ask him to telephone this number?"

There was the briefest of pauses at the other end, then the voice said, "Very well. May I tell him who is calling?"

"I—Doctor Kendall will know whom the call is from," Shane told her, and could not know that behind the distant female voice lay the thought, *I'll bet he will, and so do I.*

She waited, doing up her housework mechanically. Dee Andreas ran in for their customary midmorning coffee klatch and Shane welcomed the distraction, although it was difficult to give her attention fully to the other's rambling chatter.

Dee demanded at length, "Problems?" and when Shane looked blankly at her, "Well, you know, the body's here but the mind is absent."

"Oh, sorry, I guess I was wool-gathering. What were you saying?"

"Nothing very earthshaking. I just said I'm sorry I ever learned to read. Every time I get my hands on a new cookbook I go into orbit. I'm trying out this torte—it's ten stories high and lousy with calories. If it comes off I'll bring you a piece. If I blow it, I'll probably shoot myself. You wouldn't believe the cost of the ingredients it calls for."

"Shane." Jeff's voice sounded so clear, so near, that he might have been in the room with her. At the sound of him she began to tremble, and she was terrified she would not be able to control her voice.

"Jeff—how are you?"

"Great. You know, I was beginning to think you wouldn't call. I'd sit here and look at my phone. 'It's daytime,' I'd think. 'She should be at home alone now, or if she isn't, if she can't talk, I can always pretend I reached a wrong number.' How is everything with you?"

"Fine." She breathed deeply. "Just fine." No good. Her voice wobbled badly.

"Shane, are you crying?"

"No. Yes, maybe a little. It's just that it's good to hear your voice."

"It's no good there, is it?"

"It's all right, Jeff. Really—" I've made a wretched mistake. I shouldn't have called him.

"Listen to me. I've been doing a lot of thinking. Shane, are you listening to me?"

"Yes, Jeff."

"I should never have let you go the way you did, as if everything were over. It isn't, you know. I want to see you, Shane. I'm coming out there."

"Jeff," she was crying now, the tears streaming unchecked across her cheeks. "*Dearest* Jeff, no. You mustn't come."

"Why mustn't I?"

"Because—I don't know, it's too soon. Maybe I can come there again, in a little while. When things are—when it's really over."

"No good. There are things we left unsaid. I want us to say them now and I want us to be looking at each other when we say them. Can you meet me?"

"Jeff, please, I can't *think!*"

"Then let me do the thinking. I'll catch the early flight on Friday morning, the one you took. Will he be at work then?"

"Yes, but—"

"What time does that flight reach there?"

"Ten-thirty."

"What's the name of a hotel near the airport, where you can get in touch with me?"

"The Park Ellyn is nearby."

"I'll telephone for reservations. If I can't get them there, I'll leave word with them where I can be reached. There's a flight out of Tarant at two-thirty but it wouldn't give us time. Look, by eleven-thirty I'll be at this Park Ellyn, or they will know where I am. Shane?"

"Yes—" She was trying to corral her frightened, scurrying thoughts. Say something—*Stop him!*

"I love you." Then he was gone and there was only the humming of an empty line against her ear. Slowly she replaced the instrument. A slight sound made her turn. Through the open hall doorway she saw Dee Andreas going quietly through the kitchen toward the patio. She said, sharply, "Dee!" and the other turned. "How long have you been here?"

"I brought over a piece of the cake. You were busy on the phone so I just walked in. If you mean did I hear something I shouldn't have, I suppose I did, but I've forgotten what it was. Don't worry about it." She would have gone away then, but Shane said more quietly, "Please, come and sit down. I think I need to talk to someone."

Dee's glance was wary. "I'd rather not hear anything you'd be sorry you told me. I've always liked you, and your business is your own. I'm not about to peddle it, if that bothers you."

"I really do want to talk to you." Shane's tone still wavered on the edge of tears, and the other relented a trifle.

"Well, okay. I could do with a cup of coffee and you look like you could, too. You sit, and I'll fix it. You look like a slight breeze could blow you over."

Obediently, Shane sat at the bar. Dee opened a cupboard and got out the instant coffee jar, brought out cups and saucers. "Sorry if I put the chill on you, but it sounded like you thought I was deliberately listening in. I was trying to slip out so you wouldn't know I had been here at all, but then I forgot the damned cake—that would've blown it anyhow." Ruefully she gestured toward a large slice of gaudily frosted confection reposing in its wrapping on the bar. She brought Shane a steaming cup. "There you go. Just like in the soap operas."

"I'm sorry?"

"Oh, you know, whenever there's something heavy going down, the characters all sit around the kitchen table, drink coffee, and talk it over."

"I do want to tell you, but I don't know where to begin."

"Well, where did it begin? At the lake?"

Shane nodded, mutely.

"So you went on a vacation and you met a guy. It happens. I guess it could happen to anybody, given the right time and the right chance. How serious was it?"

"Serious enough. I—had an affair with him."

Dee nodded. "Figures. You aren't the type to flirt around just for the hell of it. He in town?"

"He will be, day after tomorrow."

"Does he want to marry you?"

"We never discussed marriage. When I left Tarant I thought that was the end of it; I honestly did." She rubbed wearily at her forehead. "His name is Jeff. Doctor Jeffrey Kendall."

"A doctor, no less!"

"A psychology professor."

"Married?"

"No."

"Did he know you are?"

"Yes." She flushed. "Please understand though, he's no part of my trouble with Court. That's been going on for a long while."

"Well, I can buy that, I guess. Art always says it's seldom a third party breaks up a marriage that wasn't on the rocks already. I hate to see it happen to you and Court, though. I'll admit I wondered a little sometimes, what with you so edgy and worn down and him so glum. Happy wasn't exactly the word I'd have used to describe you—not that it was any of my business. Tell me, does Court know about any of this?"

"No. We've had trouble since I came home, but it had nothing to do with this. Dee, you've been a good friend, and I'm sorry if I've disappointed you. I'm sure you think it was terribly wrong of me, having an affair—"

"Listen, I'm no one to decide what's wrong or right. I used to have this aunt, she was a religious *nut*. I mean really, she thought everything was wrong; drinking, cards, movies—you name it and she was against it. Of course, she had four or five husbands, so there must have been something she enjoyed, but she'd never have been caught doing it standing up, for fear someone would accuse her of dancing," and she nodded with satisfaction as Shane laughed, reluctantly. "That's better—now at least you don't look like you're on your way to an execution. Look—it's your life and you're the one who has to live it. I know what it's like to have a marriage you just can't hack any longer. I guess it doesn't make any real difference what the reason is; if you can't, you can't. I never knew Court well enough to have any idea what kind of guy he'd be to live with. It seemed to me from what I could see across the fence he was a type lots of women would give their eyeteeth for—hard working, a good provider—and

235

he doesn't make passes at every skirt that wiggles in front of him. But it takes a wife to know the truth. She's the one who stays in there with him after the drapes are pulled."

"Court is a fine man and in his own way he's never been anything but kind to me. It isn't even that I don't love him anymore—I do, at least in a way. But there are differences in us that go too deep, and I don't think things are going to get any better. I have tried, but it's not good."

"What will you do?"

"I don't know; I haven't thought that far ahead. I have the place on Shadow Lake, and some money of my own—I don't know yet."

"Well," Dee slid off her stool, patted Shane's arm a trifle awkwardly, "hang in there, baby. I hope everything works out for you. If I said anything, well, I'm no judge and jury. When the guy upstairs says 'Come forth and get your heavenly reward,' I'll probably come fifth and get a bucket of hot coals. I'm no one to say what someone else should do. You're a nice gal, and I'm all for you. If this Jeff Kendall is what you want—" Then she gestured toward the cake on the bar. "You throw that in the garbage can, I'll sue you. It only *looks* poison. If I can cook it, you can eat it."

Casey was driving Jeff to the airport, sending

her car at a fast clip through the deserted early-morning streets. Her face was pale and there were circles beneath her eyes.

Jeff said regretfully, "You look done in. I shouldn't have agreed to let you take me to the plane. I could have driven my own car and left it at the terminal."

"It's all right. I fancied this way of saying good-bye."

"Well, I'll probably be back before you've much more than finished waving your farewells." He gave her a thoughtful sidewise glance but his tone was matter-of-fact.

"I won't be here when you get back."

"I see. Well, God knows you've every right to decide that. There's not much more I can say to you, is there?"

"Not much except good-bye."

Not since I took that telephone call the other day, and not since I saw your face when you came out of the office after returning the call.

"I know my leaving so abruptly will inconvenience you, and I'm sorry about that, but Kay Marks is capable and she knows a lot about my job. She should be able to take over my duties without too much difficulty, until you decide on someone permanent."

The car crossed an almost-empty parking lot, drew up before the lighted windows of the small terminal waiting room. Casey cut the motor. It had begun to rain a little, drumming gently on the roof.

Inside the terminal only a few people moved about. There would not be many passengers for the early flight.

Jeff said, "I think the coffee shop is open. We've time for a quick breakfast."

"Thanks, I'd rather not."

"Just like this, then."

"Just like this. You'll find everything in order. All the midterm registration papers are done for all courses, and Kay knows the filing system."

"Damn the filing system! I know you've made up your mind to go and I won't try to talk you out of it—but I want you to know how rotten it makes me feel, knowing I've hurt you. You mean a great deal to me."

"I know that, and I'm being a lousy loser. The ironic part of it is that I never really had anything to lose. I knew the rules and I was willing to play by them. Well, I've had it with games! Do you want to hear something funny? I'm going to pray to whatever God it is I'm not even sure I believe in, to send me a nice guy who'll love me and fight with me and take care of me. I'm going to get me a mortgage, and some kids—" Jeff had never seen her cry but she was battling against tears now, her lips grimly compressed. After a moment she said, tautly, "I'm behaving like a lovesick teenager. I know you can't help feeling the way you do about her any more than I can help the way I feel about you. You'd better go. You'll miss your plane."

When he was near the entrance he heard her call his name. She came swiftly toward him, stumbling a little on the wet dark concrete.

"Jeff, I do love you!" Her voice was anguished. "I am so damned tired of the games people play, never saying what they really feel because it's dumb—"

He said in a gentle shamed voice, "I know."

"I want to say it all. I love you enough to want you to be happy, no matter what. If I say I hope things work out for you and her, will you believe me?"

"Yes."

"I hope they do work out. That's all. It's what I wanted you to know." Then she turned and went away from him for the last time.

It was shortly before one when Shane telephoned the Park Ellyn. A brisk masculine voice informed her, "No, madam, Doctor Kendall has not checked in. We do have a reservation for him, and if you'd care to leave a message—"

"Thank you, no message." *I should never have agreed to meet him, and if he has decided not to* come, it's for the best. Only he might have let me know.

Perhaps he was coming, though. Maybe she had called too soon. If he missed the limousine to the hotel and had trouble getting a taxi—

She went back through the hallway, hearing three chimes sound softly. Through the doorway she could see Dee.

Oh, please, not now, I don't want to talk to anyone now!

Dee's customary breezy greeting was not forthcoming. She said, abruptly, "Have you had any of the local TV stations on?"

"No, why?"

Dee pushed the bright hair from her forehead with a distracted gesture. "God. I didn't know whether to come over here or not. Listen, your guy—Doctor Jeffrey Kendall, from Tarant College—"

"Yes?" Apprehension doubled a tiny fist in the pit of her stomach. "Dee, what?"

"There was a bad crash at Municipal a couple of hours ago. It's on the air now."

Shane went into the living room, Dee trailing her. She switched on the set and almost at once the familiar face of a local newscaster filled the screen and his familiar voice, solemn with portent, filled the room:

"... mobile unit standing by to bring you all

developments as soon as they reach us. Twenty-five passengers and the crew of five are known dead, but names are being withheld pending notification of next of kin. The survivors, whose names were released earlier, and all of whom are said to be in serious condition, have been taken to City General Hospital. Authorities say it is too early to conjecture as to the cause of the crash, but eyewitnesses noted that the plane appeared to be functioning normally as it approached the runway for a landing, then seemed to falter, and plunged nose downward—"

Shane switched the set off. Dee said, "They gave his name. Doctor Jeffrey Kendall. He's one of the survivors."

In the stillness Shane could hear the ticking of a clock. She thought blankly, There is only one clock in this house that ticks and it's in the kitchen. I never knew before that one can hear it from here.

She looked down at her apron, began to untie it. "I'll have to change my dress. Will you call me a cab? I'll be ready by the time it gets here."

"You're going to the hospital?"

"Yes, but I want to get there quickly and I don't think I'd better try to drive."

"Forget the cab. I'll take you."

The nurse was an elderly woman, weary,

austere. She asked, "Are you a relative?"

"No, a friend." Shane moistened dry lips. "A very close friend. Would it be possible for me to see him?"

"I'm sorry."

"Then if someone could just let him know I'm here."

"I'm sorry," the woman said again. She looked at Shane's drawn face and hesitated, her glance going to Dee, who stood beside her friend. She shook her head slightly, and Dee nodded.

"Honey," she put a hand on Shane's arm, "don't you understand?"

"He's dead?" Shane stood very still. "That's it, isn't it? Jeff is dead."

The nurse said, "Perhaps you can speak to the doctor for a moment. We've been in touch with your friend's people—I understand someone is flying in from his home at five-thirty."

"That would be Father Francis. Jeff has no other family." She looked at the big clock above the desk. The hands stood at two. "I want to wait for him."

Dee protested, "Do you think you should?"

"You go on home. I'll stay."

The nurse gestured. "There's a lounge just down the corridor; you can wait there. Would you like the doctor to stop in—?"

"No." Shane looked blankly at her. "Thank

you. What could the doctor tell me except that he is dead?"

She walked along the corridor with Dee. "I could have kept it from happening." Her voice was drained. "I was frightened when he said he was coming. All I had to do was tell him not to come, that I couldn't see him—"

She sank into a chair in the lounge, leaning back and closing her eyes. Dee hovered anxiously.

"Listen to me. What has happened is a terrible thing and I think I know how you must be feeling, but there's nothing you can do here. Court will go home and you won't be there, and he'll ask questions."

"Then I'll answer them."

"Yeah. That's what I'm afraid of. Listen, I'm going to call the bar and tell Art you and I are downtown together and we may be a little late. I'll ask him to go over when Court gets home and tell him not to worry, that you're with me. All right?"

"All right. It doesn't matter."

"Maybe it doesn't matter this minute, but I hope to God I can talk some sense into you before we get home. I'll be right back."

In the late afternoon Father Francis paused beside the open lounge door. A girl was with him, a tall dark-haired girl whose eyelids were red and swollen from weeping. Dee saw them and hurried out.

"You're Father Doheny?"

"Yes." He looked past her at the small huddled figure in the chair beside the window. "They told me someone was waiting and I knew it must be Shane."

"She's been sleeping for a little while."

Their voices aroused Shane, who arose and came toward them. She said, brokenly, "Oh, Father Francis," and he took her hands in his.

"I know, my dear; it's a dreadful thing for all of us. Shane, this is Megan Casey, Jeffrey's secretary. Megan—"

"I know who Mrs. Manning is." There was loathing in the girl's glance, the downward drag of her lips. She swung on her heel and walked away from them.

Shane said, uncertainly, "I didn't know—it seemed to me someone should be here. Was that wrong?"

"No, of course not. Megan is under a great deal of strain. When we left Tarant, we had not been told the extent of his injuries; we only knew that he was alive, and of course we hoped—" He shook his head.

Dee said, "If you folks want to talk for a little, I'll wait in the car, but Shane, I do think we should be getting home."

"I'll walk down with her." The priest smiled at the blonde woman and she nodded and hurried away. He touched Shane's arm and they began to walk, slowly.

She said, tonelessly, "You guessed—about Jeff and me, didn't you? You can say whatever you like to me. You can't possibly say anything to me that I won't be saying to myself for the rest of my life. It's because of me that he's dead. That girl—I don't recall his ever having mentioned her."

"It seems odd he wouldn't have. She's been with him for quite some time."

"She was in love with him." It was not a question.

"Very much, I think."

She shook her head. "In the time I knew Jeff, it never occurred to me to wonder if there was anyone else. Was he in love with her?"

"I don't think it is my right to discuss what may or may not have been between them." The priest's voice was not unkind, only brushed by sadness.

They walked together down a long flight of steps and came out into the main entrance lobby. Father Francis said, "Shane, I know it will not be easy to put this behind you, but it is what you must do. It's over with now, gone into the past. For my part I can pray, I do pray, that there may have been an awareness that he was about to die, even one instant of contrition—"

"Oh, my God, don't! I don't want to hear that!"

"I'm sorry. I believe; perhaps you don't. One of us has to be wrong. Jeffrey's life here is finished. I am concerned for him in the next. I want you to listen very carefully to what I am going to say. Jeffrey was an exceptional man in many ways. He also had many faults."

"Please—"

"He was a sensual man and sometimes a selfish one. There were many things about him I did not understand. I know he was concerned for his fellow man, but it was an objective concern. He insulated his own emotions carefully. I'm not saying he didn't care for you; perhaps he did. I was not in his confidence. He is gone now, but he is accountable for his own deeds. See well to *your* accountability, my dear. Go home, now, and God go with you." When she would have spoken, he said firmly, "Your friend is waiting."

She had reached the bottom of the steps leading into the street, when she heard someone calling her name. Looking back she saw the girl, Megan Casey, hurrying after her. In the doorway the priest had paused and was looking back. After a brief hesitation he shook his head and disappeared into the building. Shane waited, thinking, If she is going to accuse me I'll simply walk away. I can't bear any more.

The girl said, "Mrs. Manning, I was rude to you back there. It was rotten of me."

"It doesn't matter."

"It does to me. Jeff was honest with me about you. I knew why he was coming here, and I—told him I hoped things would work out for you and him."

"It was you who answered the telephone the day I called?"

"Yes."

"Jeff didn't tell me about you. I'm sorry for that. I didn't know we might be hurting someone."

Jeff knew, though. Then what about his philosophy that it's only a sin if you hurt someone else?

"There wasn't all that much for him to tell. We played a little game, he and I. Maybe in the beginning you and he played it. Knowing him, I'd rather imagine you did. It wasn't just some kind of rip-off with Jeff, it was just that his relationships had always had an escape hatch. It got to be different with you, only he forgot to tell you he had changed the rules. All of a sudden you were gone and he hadn't told you he loved you."

Shane said, uncertainly, "Miss Casey, I—thank

you for coming to speak to me. It can't have been easy for you."

"It was easier than you might think, once I was over being angry. You have the right to know that you are probably the only woman Jeff Kendall ever fell really in love with—but you need to know, too, that if he hadn't fallen in love with you, in the long run how you felt wouldn't have mattered. I'm not trying to make him out some sort of heel, but for your own sake, I don't think you should make him out some sort of martyr. He really wasn't, you know."

There was bewilderment in Shane's glance. "If he hadn't been on that plane, coming to me, he'd—still be alive. I know that, but I don't understand why you feel you must say these things to me?"

"Because I knew Jeff. He was on that plane because there was something *he* wanted. I think it's important for you to understand that. Just so you'll understand that it wasn't you who killed him. Good-bye, Mrs. Manning."

When they were in the car, homeward bound, Dee said, "You'd better put on some lipstick and straighten your hair. You look like you've been pulled through a knothole backward."

When Shane gave no sign that she heard, Dee

grew urgent. "Hey! I know this is rotten for you, but you've got to pull yourself together before we get home. Now is no time for making decisions, and I'd hate to see you do something that you're going to regret. I've got this lousy feeling that if Court is upset and gets on your case, you're apt to spill the whole thing. Don't do it, Shane; give yourself time to get it all together. We've been shopping, we went to a movie, you've got a splitting headache and don't feel like talking—I don't care what you tell Court, only lie like hell!"

"I'm not much good at lying."

"You'd better get good in a hurry!" Dee's words were a small explosion of sound. "Look, the guy is dead; you can't change that. What you can do is keep from blowing it until you've had a chance to think things through. Damn it, are you listening to me at all?"

Shane stirred. She opened her purse and looked inside it, searching listlessly through its contents. "We left home in such a hurry that I didn't bring anything."

"My bag is on the backseat. There's lipstick and a comb in it. Help yourself."

It was nearly eight when she came into the house. Court was there, and fuming.

"I've been worried out of my mind. If you hadn't turned up in another half hour I was going to call the police. Where in hell have you been? Of all the harebrained stunts—Why didn't you call me, or leave a note?"

She thought blankly, We're back to normal now. I've done something idiotic that he can fret about. "Didn't you see Art?"

"Yes, I saw Art, but it was hours ago that Dee called him. For all I knew you might have had car trouble and been stranded where you couldn't get to a telephone." It was the most he had talked to her in days, Shane thought, but she was too weary to be amused.

"I'm sorry, Court, but please don't shout at me. I've a wretched headache," and that was nothing but the truth. "I'll fix you some supper."

"Don't bother, I had a sandwich."

Court tiptoed into the bedroom, but Shane was awake, sitting at the dressing table brushing her hair. The reaction, she thought numbly, was setting in now. Her arms felt so leaden she could barely lift them to their task, and she was filled with dread of the moment when she must lie upon her pillow in the darkness and let her thoughts take over.

If he insists on asking any more questions I don't think I can hold out against him.

I don't care what you tell him, only lie like hell!

I can't. I don't even want to. There are so many things he and I have hidden, from ourselves, from each other—I think they are all going to have to come out.

He sat on the edge of his bed, looking at her. "I'm sorry I yelled at you." The words were mollifying but there was still anger in his tone. "But you had no business going off like that, without even leaving me a note. The way things have been with us lately—Well, anyway, maybe Art Andreas doesn't care if his wife goes chasing off until all hours, but I do. Where were you, anyway?"

Shane drew a long deep breath. "I think I'd better tell you about that. I was—at the hospital."

11.

He paced the floor, thrusting his hands agitatedly through his hair, eyes glaring at Shane from his bloodless face. She sat erect, hands folded on the glass top of the dressing table, watching him in the mirror. For long moments after her calm dispassionate voice had finished its narrative, no words were spoken.

At last Court said, hoarsely, "I don't believe you. You're out of your mind. Lying!"

"It would be a pretty stupid lie, wouldn't it? And for what purpose?" A bit of powder had spilled on the gleaming surface of her dressing table and she wiped it carefully away with a facial tissue. "He was on the plane. Now he's dead."

"Where were you going to meet him, at some hotel?" He came close to her, to stare down at her, his hand half lifted as if to strike her, but then he let it fall to his side. She stared back at him.

Go ahead and hit me—and I swear I'll pick up whatever I can lay my hands on and try to kill you!

The shock of it, her momentary need for the sheer release of physical violence, unnerved her. She turned away and put her hands to her face.

"Was Dee going to take you to the hotel, too?"

"None of this concerns Dee. She was pulled into it through no choice of her own."

"I'll just bet! She'd know the ropes, all right, a cheap broad like that!" He was lashing out at her with a kind of frenzy. "I could tell you a thing or two about her. All the time you were gone, she was always bringing stuff over here, trying to feed me. Hell, I could have taken her to bed anytime I wanted to!"

"Oh, Court, that's not true and you know it." She had to put down a wild impulse to laughter. She knew he was only trying to hurt her, but it was so silly!

Abruptly he sat down again, drawing a long shaken breath. "Some guy you'd never seen before—in just a few days you're in the hay with him." The brutal edge of his anger was draining away. "Why, Shane? Will you just tell me in the name of God, *why?*" He did not wait for a reply, but went on, his voice sounding thick and muffled, "You see it happen to other men and you think you're the lucky one; you think, 'Not my wife, she's decent and straight and I can trust her,' and you feel sorry for the poor bastard it happens to. The other night when we were talking about Brad Ellers—God! ... Why in hell did you come back, if it was him you wanted?"

"I wanted to come back. I really wanted to," and at his gesture of rejection, "It's true. I dreaded coming back—but I did feel I was beginning to understand myself a little. When I went to Shadow Lake, I needed time to think things through, but I did believe that I was going to ask you for a divorce. Maybe if I hadn't felt that way, that you and I were through—" She shrugged, futilely. "That's not an excuse; I'm just saying how it was with me. I did change my mind about the divorce. I'm not sure why, maybe I felt there just might be a chance for us."

"Then why was he coming out here? To try to talk you into leaving me again?"

"I was to blame for that. I had promised to telephone him, and I did. He sensed things were not going well for us, and he—said he wanted to talk to me. I didn't want him to come. I should have told him I didn't want him to. I'll always be sorry I didn't."

"Did he want to marry you?"

"I don't know. Maybe, at the end—We never talked about it. Jeff was a wonderful, warm human being, but he had his own ideas about things. In the beginning, I think that even if I had been divorced, he wouldn't have wanted to marry me—"

"But you let him take you in like any stupid little high-school girl."

"That's not quite the way it was. I went into it with my eyes wide open. I was aware Jeff felt he wasn't suited to marriage, the way—" she said it deliberately, "—you seemed to feel you weren't suited to fatherhood," and felt a certain grim satisfaction in seeing the dull flush darken his face. "He was honest with me, and that is something I tried very hard to learn from him, how to be honest. I was never very good at it.

Oh, in all the things that mattered to you, I was—but in some ways that mattered the very most to me, I didn't know how to be honest with myself. I suppose I lacked the courage to insist on the right to make my life the way I really wanted it to be."

She stopped speaking and after a long moment Court said, slowly, "Maybe I've hurt you in ways I didn't even know about, but this—" He went to a window, to stare out at the night with unseeing eyes. "Those things you said the other night, about my mother, and the way I was toward you. I've been trying to work it out in my mind, honestly trying to understand it. Maybe I was a damned fool for not guessing you were saying things someone else had taught you to feel."

"That's not true. I've felt that way for a very long time—as if Adele were looking over our shoulders. I should have told you how I felt, only you would never listen. It was one of the things I didn't have the courage to be honest about."

"Then tell me this. If you had really decided to stay with me—My God, Shane, why tell me at all?" There was a real anguish in him and something in Shane tried to meet it with compassion and truth.

"I think I must make you understand why I had to tell you, or we are both lost. I could have kept my secret. At first I meant to, just as I'd tried to keep it from you that I was lonely and frightened and that the things I needed most from you, you were denying me. Almost everything about us, the things you said and did, the sex part, everything, seemed to diminish me as a person until there was nothing left. Maybe I never really knew how to give, either—but I truly think I might have learned. I never wanted to hurt you. I don't now, but I don't want to *be* hurt anymore. I wanted you, or someone, to accept me for what I am and love me for it, and not to try to make me into something I don't want to be. Maybe I can't say it so it will make sense to you, but I think the thing of real value he gave me was the thing I wanted most from you, a feeling of self-worth. Can you understand that I've never had that before?"

Court moved his head from side to side, as if he were in physical pain. "Sex, that was what it was with you and him, wasn't it?"

"Not the most important part." He isn't listening. Even now, he isn't listening. "It was something I could give, I'll admit it, something I wanted to give, not just something he took as his right, without really giving a—a *damn* how I felt about it!" She thought with faint amusement that it was the first time in her life she had ever uttered a swear word.

Maybe it's time I learned how, if that's what it

takes to get the truth across.

"But he took, didn't he?" Court grew angry again. "He got what he was after. How does that make him so different?"

"I'm not talking about how he may have felt, I'm talking about how he made me feel; I'm saying that he *cared* how I felt! Is that so difficult to understand? Because if it is, Court, then we've said everything there is to say."

"Damn it, I cared how you felt, too, anyway I used to, only I guess I gave up trying to figure it. Maybe I'm not quite as thick-skinned as you seem to think. Certainly I can understand that what you're saying is that I'm a selfish slob, and this guy wasn't! Well, you might be surprised at the times I've held myself back from saying and doing things—" He chopped it off, and Shane watched him with a sudden awareness in her eyes.

She said, slowly, "Maybe you should have said and done them. How else were we to know, either of us, what the other one really wanted?"

Court stared at her, then took a restless turn about the room. "Hell, I know we haven't been all that good in bed, just as I know it's in my nature to be a little overbearing—and in yours to be a little on the cold side. At least that's what I thought." There was no reproach in his tone now, only a statement of fact. "You meant enough to me that I was willing to settle for what we had. I never cheated on you. I don't say I've never played around with the idea. I've had a few chances, and I'm not throwing that at you, I'm just telling you."

She folded her hands in her lap and looked down at them. "Maybe I'm not as much on the cold side as you think. It was one of those things you decided for me, don't you see? You decided how far we would go, before we were married, and after. It wasn't something we shared, it was—just something you did to me, and were always a little bit ashamed of."

A long silence fell between them. Court broke it at last to say, "Whatever you've done, you're a good woman, I know that. You did what you did, and maybe I'm a big part of whatever it was that drove you to it. The trouble is, I don't know if I'm big enough to accept that much of the blame."

"I'm not asking you to. I can take my own consequences. There may be—a great many of those. It isn't pleasant to realize that a man is dead because of me."

"He was coming here of his own free will."

"It isn't quite that simple. You asked me if he wanted to marry me and I gave you only part of the answer. At the last, I think that was what was in his mind. I—had an idea that was what he was coming here to talk about, and it was wrong of me, terribly wrong, to let him come. I know that, and it's a knowledge I have to live with."

"But you'd have said yes, when he asked you."

Shane looked levelly at him. "I would have said no. That's what makes it all so senseless. I loved Jeff, but I wasn't *in* love with him. I always thought that was such a trite phrase, so meaningless, but now I know what it means. So you see, there was no point in his coming, and if I had made him understand that, he'd still be alive."

"Then why?" Court's tone was heavy with disbelief. "Why did you let him come?"

"For all the wrong reasons. I was hurt and confused, and very angry with you. I wanted to lean on him for just a little longer, to have him tell me how fine and rewarding life can be if only one has the courage to be oneself. I think I was angry, too, because I knew that I was going to refuse what he offered. I couldn't really be in love with him because I had never quite gotten over being in love with you. That's pretty funny, isn't it?" She was swaying with weariness now, her head throbbing. "You can despise me for this, but I think if I hadn't met Jeff, and loved him in whatever way it was that I loved him, then I would never have realized that I am still in love with you."

He said, woodenly, "You love me, Shane?"

"Yes, only I don't know what to do about it now."

She arose then and left the room, closing the door behind her, going slowly along the shadowy hallway. In the living room she groped her way to a chair and sank into it, feeling her body sway as if she were at the tip of a vast pendulum.

For a little bit back there, I felt brave and strong, as if somehow the truth could make us both whole. Now there is nothing. Jeff is dead, and I may have destroyed Court.

Had everything she said been the truth? When had she really known that she was not truly in love with Jeff? He had given her so much, so much—

It was a game he played. The girl—Casey, was that her name?—had said that.

Hadn't Shane believed, from the beginning, that it was only a game both of them were playing?

If he hadn't fallen in love with you, how you felt wouldn't really have mattered. The girl had said that, too, and in her voice had been the grieving bitterness of one who knew.

When I came home, if things could have been the way I hoped, between Court and me, then I could have said to Jeff, "No, I don't want you to come." I think that I would not have telephoned him at all.

Dear God, how selfish we are, all of us!

He was on that plane because there was something he wanted. If I had said I didn't want to see him, would he have insisted on coming, anyway?

Just so you'll understand it wasn't you who killed him.

Oh, God, I want to believe that!

Please.

Her tormented thoughts spun themselves out into oblivion. Her head dropped, and she slept. She awakened just before dawn, with the gray light beginning to come dimly through the big window.

Footsteps sounded in the hallway and Court said, "Shane?"

"I'm here."

He came toward her, standing hesitantly near. "Do you know what you want to do?"

"No. If you'd rather I left, I can go back to Shadow Lake. It doesn't matter." Only I won't go back there and hide. I'll find a way to pick up the pieces; I'll finish school—something.

"I've been sitting in there all night, thinking. Sometimes it came rolling over me like a black cloud, then I wanted to hurt you the way you were hurting me. I wanted to call you filthy names."

"I know."

"Then I'd think how it would be if I lost you. It kept coming back to that. I don't want to lose you. I wish I could say I understand what you've done. I could try. If I try—would it work, Shane?"

"I honestly don't know. I don't know how fully either of us could accept what the other tried to give, now."

"Well, neither of us knew how it would work when we first decided to get married, did we?" He gave a little laugh, forced and unnatural, and his pathetic attempt at humor tore at her more painfully than his most righteous anger could have done.

"I don't know what to say to you, Court. Everything would be so different now. You'd have bad times, and I couldn't play the part of a penitent, humbly accepting punishment. I'm sorry I've hurt you. I'm sorry we've hurt each other. But we'd have to go on from there and let the past go. I'm not sure we could."

"I understand what you're saying, and I know it wouldn't be easy, but mightn't it be worth trying? Maybe we could get help—from one of those marriage counselors. I'd be willing, if you wanted it that way." He said it awkwardly and his very awkwardness betrayed the despairing need in him. "I guess there's a lot we don't know about each other, or about ourselves either, for that matter. Those things you said about me—I know you were right about a lot of them and maybe I couldn't change them overnight, but I could begin. I love you, you know that. You said you love me."

"You'd have to know that. It's no good unless you know."

"All right, I know." He knelt beside her, touching her hand lying on the arm of the chair, then withdrawing quickly as if afraid his touch might offend her. "Oh, God, Shane, can't we just *try?*"

She felt his tears dropping on her hand, and she thought she must surely be unable to draw a breath against the pain in her.

"Yes." For the moment there was nothing in her except the pain—no fear, no hope, only the pain. Then there was the faint beginning knowledge that it was what she wanted, too. "Yes. We can try."

12.

Casey thought, What am I doing here? I shouldn't have come. She looked numbly about her at the somber faces.

The day had turned out to be unseasonably warm, and in the crowded chapel the air was oppressive. Sunlight beat through the windows;

dust motes danced lazily in the brilliant shafts. A wasp, heavy with autumn sluggishness, was trapped against a pane, and Casey watched as it alternately struggled to escape through the glass and fell back to the sill to lie with its legs thrashing futilely, making a small droning sound.

Although the chapel was filled, the seats to either side of Casey were vacant. People had stayed away from them, as if they were reserved for mourners who had not yet arrived.

Doctor Frank Rogers stood at the lectern, speaking quietly. Only random words penetrated the turmoil in Casey's mind. *Young—friend of the young—forward-looking—*

If there had to be a eulogy by a faculty member, probably better Doctor Rogers than anyone else. Of them all, Jeff had liked and respected him the most.

She could not focus her attention on the words. Weariness was like a drug in her, making her feel as sluggish as the insect which droned intermittently in the small silences between Doctor Rogers's words. She had had scant sleep since the flight home, two days ago. She had come alone, Father Francis having left directly from California, accompanying Jeff's body back to its final resting place beside his parents.

Jeff's body . . . his cold dead body . . . the body of the deceased . . . Oh, God, when does the hurt begin?

Father Francis had telephoned back to the campus, so she had been spared witnessing the first shock wave which stunned them. She received the quiet subdued condolences of Jeff's faculty members courteously, without resentment. Many of them had not liked him, some of them had been his academic enemies, but none of them would have wished him harm.

It was the students who insisted on a memorial service in the chapel, where neither Jeff nor many of them had ever attended. It was not a church service; it was only a farewell. He would never be coming back to Tarant campus, but it was unthinkable that he simply depart from them without their saying their good-byes.

Doctor Rogers finished speaking and sat down. From the front row a boy arose and walked to the lectern. He was Randy Bedaker, who had led the rebellion against compulsory attendance in this very chapel.

"I feel more honored than I can tell you," his voice was breathy and ragged with emotion, and very young, "at being the student chosen by you to speak here. Doctor Kendall was my friend—"

Exhaustion was catching up with Casey now, and something more shattering, an awareness of the dreadful finality of the words being spoken here. She began to tremble badly and she slid her hands, palms downward, beneath her, in a desperate attempt to steady her body.

The trembling grew worse and young Bedaker's voice swam in and out of her consciousness, without always clarifying into words which were distinguishable to her.

My God, am I going to faint? I have never fainted in my life.

"We'll remember him long after we've forgotten all the others—"

Please don't let me make a fool of myself!

Dimly she was aware that someone had come quietly into the seat next to her. A supporting arm went about her shoulders and a hand took hers, firmly.

"Steady on." It was Ted Dunlap's whisper, close to her ear. "It's nearly over with, now."

Presently the service ended and people began stirring about. Dunlap said, "We'll wait until the crowd thins out," and she nodded, grateful for his supporting arm, and did not notice when a few faculty members approached, to be motioned away by a slight shake of the coach's head. Students passed by, looking at Casey with sorrowing eyes, then hurried on.

She asked, in a low voice, "How did you know?"

"I was watching you."

"Do you think the others noticed?"

"I don't know. Does it matter?"

"No."

When the chapel had nearly emptied, they arose. Near the front a lonely figure was still seated, a girl whose face was puffy from weeping, her eyes red rimmed. Casey said, "There's Maryanne Anderson. I must speak to her."

Oh, Jeff, you left so many things unfinished!

The girl looked up dully as they approached. "Hello, Casey, Mr. Dunlap."

"Hello, Maryanne. Look, can you come to my apartment this evening? I want to talk to you." And as the other hesitated, her glance turning wary, "Jeff wanted us to talk. I promised him."

"I—all right. I'll come."

Casey walked with the coach through the bright autumn sunlight toward her car. He asked, "Have you decided what you're going to do now? Are you staying on?"

"No. As a matter of fact, I'd already given notice before Jeff—before. I'm going to Riverton. I won't have any difficulty finding a position there, and it's where Turnaround is, and the headquarters for the hotline. Both had been depending on him for a great deal of help and advice. I helped him set up the programs and I'm familiar with them. Maybe I can help." They had reached her car now and stood facing each other. "I'll be leaving in a couple of days, as soon as I can get my things ready to ship. If Maryanne agrees, I may try to find an apartment with an extra bedroom, so when she has to leave here she can stay with me until she decides what she wants to do. Maybe she can learn to handle a hotline phone. It would give her something to occupy her mind."

"What about you? Are you going to be all right?"

"I'll be fine. Oh, I'll lie me down and bleed a little—but then I'll get up and pick up the pieces and put them back together. One of these days you won't even be able to see where the mended places are.... When I'm settled in somewhere, I'll let you know. Will you call me sometimes?"

He shook his head. "I don't think so, Megan. You call me—if you ever need me—or want me."

Casey nodded, and put out a hand. He took it briefly. Then she got into her car and drove away.